THE WHITE REVI[E]

C000001518

29

Solace CALEB AZUMAH NELSON 11

Interview SCHOLASTIQUE MUKASONGA 20

Art HERVÉ GUIBERT 28

Boys BRANDON TAYLOR 51

Poetry LAURA ELLIOTT 65

The Secret Country of Her Mind EMILY BERRY 73

Interview INGRID POLLARD 95

Poetry JENNIFER LEE TSAI 117

Woman with a White Pekingese ELIZABETH O'CONNOR 121

Interview FANNY HOWE 138

Poetry JACK UNDERWOOD 147

Art ADAM PENDLETON 153

Two Stories ILYA LEUTIN *tr.* ANNA ASLANYAN 169

On Water VICTORIA ADUKWEI BULLEY 177

CORVI-MORA

2020

Alison Britton
17 September–31 October

Alvaro Barrington
5 November – 22 December

2021

Gordon Baldwin
January – February

Colter Jacobsen
February – March

Sam Bakewell
March – May

Rob Barnard, Robert Burnier & Julian Stair
May-June

Jennifer Packer
June –July

Corvi-Mora
1a Kempsford Road, London, SE11 4NU
telephone 020 7840 9111 facsimile 020 7840 9112
www.corvi-mora.com

Dana Schutz

Shadow of a Cloud Moving Slowly

16 September - 19 December 2020

3 & 11 Duke Street

St James's

London, SW1Y 6BN

www.thomasdanegallery.com

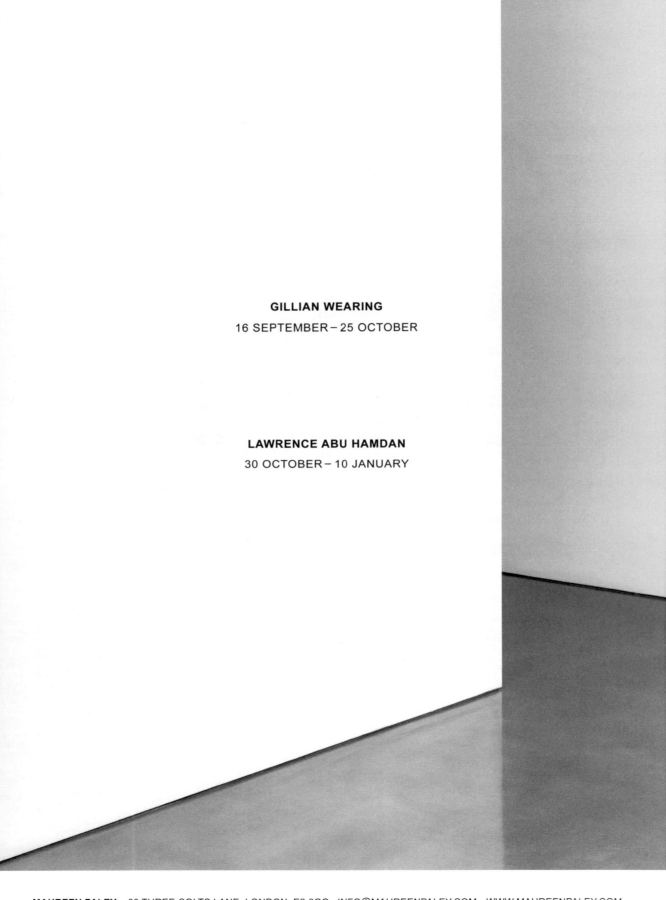

GILLIAN WEARING
16 SEPTEMBER – 25 OCTOBER

LAWRENCE ABU HAMDAN
30 OCTOBER – 10 JANUARY

Matthew Barney
Cosmic Hunt

Visit site
cosmichunt.sadiecoles.com

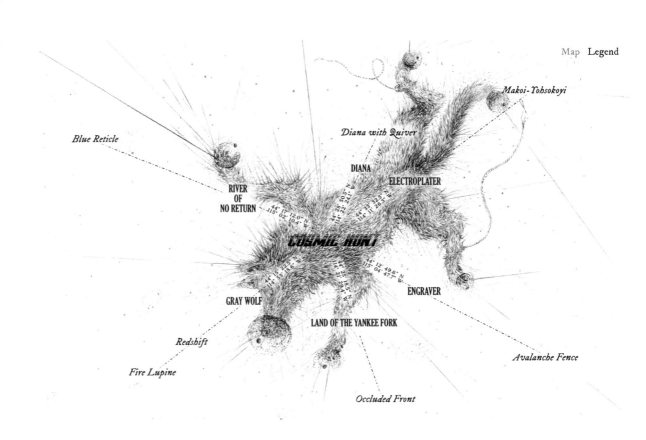

Map Legend

Rein Gold by Elfriede Jelinek
(tr. Gitta Honegger) is published
by Fitzcarraldo Editions on
13 January 2021.

'In *Rein Gold*, Jelinek reimagines the characters
of Brunhilde and Wotan from Wagner's Ring
Cycle and transposes them into the context
of modernity. She delivers an impassioned exposé
of the discontents of capitalism. Her musical thought
is interwoven with myth, politics, and Wagnerian
motifs. Gitta Honegger's excellent translation
allows us to experience the intense flow of her
characters' streams of consciousness entangled
in greed and alienation.'
— Xiaolu Guo, author of *A Lover's Discourse*

Fitzcarraldo Editions

MARY WEATHERFORD

Train Yards
Through December 19, 2020
20 Grosvenor Hill, London

MELEKO MOKGOSI

Democratic Intuition
Through December 12, 2020
6–24 Britannia Street, London

NATHANIEL MARY QUINN

Through November 21, 2020
17–19 Davies Street, London

GAGOSIAN

Published by The White Review, November 2020
Edition of 1,000

Printed in the U.K.
Typeset in Nouveau Blanche

ISBN No. 978-1-9160351-2-6
The White Review is a registered charity (number 1148690)

The White Review, 8–12 Creekside, London SE8 3DX
www.thewhitereview.org

EDITORIAL

Within this issue, writers and artists reckon with histories both personal and political, and explore the possibilities for creating sense – and even beauty – from loss and suffering. Several of the pieces that follow are united by an interest in image-making, and the political implications of placing another subject before a lens. In her polyvocal account of agoraphobia, which traverses the effects of fear on place, time, dreams and imagination, Emily Berry quotes Ariella Azoulay, who argues that the subject of a photograph imagines a future in which someone sees their suffering and takes action. Ingrid Pollard – who is interviewed in this issue, and provides its cover – uses portraiture and landscape photography to challenge racist ideologies of nationalism and heritage; by placing in the foreground figures usually deemed invisible, her work lets her subjects feel, as Caleb Azumah Nelson writes here in relation to his own photographic work, that they are 'not being looked at, but seen'.

Language, Ngũgĩ wa Thiong'o has written, 'is the collective memory bank of a people's experience in history': in a powerful and moving interview, Scholastique Mukasonga describes how she began writing following the persecution of the Rwandan Tutsis, out of a fear of forgetting, and 'to answer the call of my dead'. Her novels and memoirs, she writes here, are born from mourning: they are 'paper graves that I had to build for my family and for every victim who, lost in the genocide's anonymity, remains unburied'. Nelson's essay 'Solace' seeks its own language for mourning, moving from a private experience of grief to the 'mourning Black people experience on a global scale'. 'It is hard to dream', writes Nelson, 'when you are always so close to death'. In 'On Water', Victoria Adukwei Bulley explores the coastlines of West Africa and Brazil, where the aftereffects of the transatlantic slave trade can still be felt. She uncovers the material and emotional resonance of colonial history: lands excavated in search of profits, people and histories displaced, languages imposed. Bulley and Nelson have discovered that they share a distant ancestor; read together, these essays enact a material evocation of the sense of community to which each writer is giving voice.

In the issue's fiction, Ilya Leutin's wry 'Dictators' Hands' offers a grisly warning to those in power; Brandon Taylor's story 'Boys' skewers racism, homophobia and white liberal guilt through the eyes of a young man working in an Iowa deli, while Elizabeth O'Connor's 'Woman with a White Pekingese' delves into the murky world of dog shows, where tensions run high and no one – human or animal – is quite who they seem. The winner of the White Review Short Story Prize 2020, O'Connor's work was praised by the judges for its 'stylistic precision, terse dialogue, morbid humour and ultimate emotional cut'. As a dismal summer shifts to an uncertain winter, readers seeking sources of hope may take succour from American poet Fanny Howe's response to the question 'When are you happy?': 'The safety of an ended day, with children around, beds open, a friend whirling ice around in her glass, music on the box, puzzlement.'

SOLACE
CALEB AZUMAH NELSON

ESSAY

I lost my faith the year my Grandma passed away. She was here and then she was not, and my belief slipped away with similar ease. It was a year in which loss was rife: an aunt had passed several months before, and almost a month to the day later, another died suddenly, leaving behind a husband and toddler. I watched something break in both father and son. The boy stopped speaking and could only communicate his grief in actions. He was always opening and closing cupboards and doors, as if he was looking for his mother, or maybe he understood, and was searching for a space large enough to house his ache.

The day my Grandma died, something in me broke. I spent a long time not knowing how to say this, not knowing what language there was to say this, not knowing that it was okay to say this. I spent a long time not knowing. The only thing I know now is that I will spend eternity not knowing. There are no answers, but there are ways to cope.

Instead of language, an image: at the funeral of my aunt, standing slightly to the side as the casket was lowered into the ground. Watching my uncle take some crumbling earth in a closed fist, and hearing it scatter on the casket like light rain. Other family members were invited to do the same. Each fistful of soil felt like a soft hand against a door, knocking, knocking, knocking – knowing there could be no answer.

On the first day, my mother paced the house. She swept the corners of our living room, gathering all she could. I could see that with this simple act she was reaching into the corners of her own mind, gathering all she could there too, hoping not to forget. We had a small service in the same room a few days later, during which the pastor assured us that death was not the end. He was right. Time had taken on a different, hazy quality in which we seemed locked in stasis, moving in place. The days stretched, accented with memorial services and meals and cousins gathered on stairs, in hallways, and one aunt, a semi-permanent fixture, placing a tender palm to my elbow, always asking if I wanted a Supermalt. I would hold the cold bottle, swallowing, swallowing the ache. How it ached. When the limbo cleared, this is what remained. There was before and there was after, but I could only think of it as a time preparing for the ache, and that thing throbbing in my chest.

During that time, my mother asked me to film as people came in and out of our house, paying their respects. Through my lens, I caught glimpses of at least fifty people, friends and family. Some stayed for minutes, some stayed for days. Everyone wore black against a coloured canvas. I filmed the majority of this time with a camera stabiliser, so when I watched the footage back, each frame was like a daydream, the camera drifting through this limbo. I had plans to make a film cutting up the footage of our London home with images from the last time I was in Ghana, over fifteen years ago, but my hard drive failed. The images I had filmed of my Grandma many years before, sitting on a stool in a full kitchen, chopping onions and garlic in preparation for a stew, were lost. The images I had filmed more recently of my parents, sitting in our back garden in a purple dusk, holding hands just after they had finished praying, my mother teary, my father telling her that it was going to be okay, were lost. The images of the pastor in our living room, assuring us that death was not the end, were lost. I had sought solace in expression, and lost this too. The mourning continued.

In the year after my maternal Grandma passed, my parents sought solace in the church. They sought solace in familiarity and a stable place to hold their faith, in the face of a life they had been so sure of, crumbling.

For my parents, prayer serves as a form of expression, a place for their innermost desires to emerge. My mother can be heard at the same time every day, just before lunchtime, praying for her sons or her daughter or her husband or her family; I see her sometimes, lost in the throes, really going for it, like a rapper in the booth, freestyling, hearing the sly smile in their voice as their truth rises to the surface, or a painter knowing the strokes are correct as they come. I see her sometimes, and know she is doing something honest.

I never saw it, but I know that the church my parents attend started in a living room in Peckham, where a group of West Africans, far from home, needed a house for their faith. They needed to believe there was something better, something more, than freezing winters and the longing for the comfort of home. I imagine a plush carpet, furniture with plastic covers, thermostat turned up high. The customary hi-fi in a corner playing gospel, the volume low as they prayed, littered with phrases such as *where two or three are gathered, there you are in our midst*. I imagine a group of people reaching for their innermost desires in a space where they could ask for anything. I imagine that when they were done, they would dish out food prepared with care, someone heaving jollof onto paper plates, drinks poured, laughter, unbridled joy, the music louder now. Perhaps they would gather around the TV for football on a Sunday afternoon, each person invested in the match, even if it was not their home team. I imagine comfort. A home away from home. I imagine community. I imagine freedom.

These spaces are beautiful acts of defiance. Three years since my Grandma passed, I continue to wrangle with my own faith, but cannot negate the necessity of church community to Black people. These spaces are not without flaws. They often reflect the systems which oppress: an institution employing a hierarchical structure, where gender still rules and power remains the currency of choice. But I gaze at my parents and see the Church as a place where they might gather with others and not have to explain themselves. Where they can engage a community and see themselves. Where they can feel beautiful. Where they might feel free.

This freedom emerges from acts of refusal. Through ritual, such as the praise and worship in which a congregation might become so frenzied they approach ecstasy, or in the breaking of bread and sharing of refreshments after a service. This freedom emerges in the quiet, the quotidian, the practices which have become the everyday, actions which, according to the scholar Tina Campt, register on a deeper, lower frequency, meaning these quotidian practices, in addition to being seen and heard, are things that can be felt. Campt's work focuses on quiet and interiority as a metaphor for the life Black people live in full, beyond public stereotypes, a life which taps into our desires, our vulnerabilities, our truths. The interior is understood to be the source of human action, *a choice, a place one surrenders to, rather than going to after rejection*: a place to which we lead ourselves, rather than one we're forced towards. A place of quiet. Silence usually comes about from suppression or repression, or having to withhold: it is absence, it is stillness. It is being looked at and not seen. Quiet, in this instance, is something different altogether: it is presence, fullness, it is motion; it is ritual, it is frenzy, it is ecstasy.

And this kind of life is an act of refusal.

Refusal is a heavy practice, considering what lies on the other side.

Refusal is a necessary practice, considering what lies on the other side.

Refusal means everything when to refuse brings you closer to freedom.

I was raised in the church. I was raised in a place where Black people converged upon whatever space would hold them – a community hall, an industrial warehouse, someone's living room – and would praise and worship and say things that were honest and true, God-like even, to themselves or to others. I was raised in a place in which Black people built small worlds for themselves to exist within; in which they could refuse daily atrocities and unrest; in which they could love and feel free.

I was raised in the church, but I lost my faith the year my Grandma passed away. My own personal grief became something much larger in the context of a collective grief, a mode of mourning Black people experience on a global scale, which overcame any belief I had in anything, really. I could not see. I could not hear. I could not feel. I did not write. I did not pray – I could not pray. But I know what it means to pray. I know what it means to speak a truth and go towards it, through words or actions. I know what it means to raise your hands, not in surrender to an early demise, but in surrender to your freedom.

I saw this freedom one Sunday, that glorious Sunday, a few days after my Grandma had passed, in my parents' family church, now housed in a building in Forest Hill. A group of men came over to where I stood with my family during praise and worship, when the drums were at their quickest and the bassist plucked notes I could feel in my chest, and with these sounds, the melodies, the percussion, the bass, we, the congregation, approached frenzy. The men took each of my father's arms and led him to the front. He danced, how he danced! I saw him turning with the ease of a child, his face contorted in cheeky disdain, taunting his dancing part- ner (a man of similar age); I saw the pair of them waving handkerchiefs, moving with such little effort, watching my father move past pleasure into joy; I saw him unlock a part of his identity he doesn't entertain all that often. I saw him free.

To show up on Sunday for a service is a prayer in itself; a display of faith in something better, something more. A Black congregation engages in the collective dream of their freedom. It is hard to dream when you are always so close to death. Gathered together, seated in twos and threes, this is a room full of God-like beings, trying to be honest, reaching towards something further, deeper; reaching towards themselves. There is a cultivated safety that encourages truth. There is a cultivated safety that encourages surrender.

And when was the last time you surrendered? What Church have you built yourself where you can surrender? And what does it mean to surrender in this position, so close to death, always needing to protect, always needing to survive? What does it mean to dream when you know a grief so extraordinary, it's hard to imagine healing?

It is hard, as a Black person, to feel safe in the face of extraordinary grief. We are all mourning. The grief is extraordinary. It is difficult to comprehend such loss when it goes unspoken. It is difficult to comprehend such loss when it does not stop.

*

British rule in Ghana ended in 1957, when Ghana achieved independence within the Commonwealth. The gold jewellery and artefacts looted during colonial rule, between 1867 and Ghana's independence, remain in possession of the British and are housed in various museums and gallery spaces across the UK. Much of this gold was acquired during a British Punitive Expedition to Kumasi in 1874, whose primary motivation was to gain control of gold and slaves. Following pushback from the Asante people, an army was deployed to prevent the British from seizing the area surrounding the Elmina settlement, which they had purchased from the Dutch. With a war impending and negotiations failing, the British commander, Sir Garnet Wolseley, gave orders to ransack Kumasi; several days later, after having taken all they could, the town was burned down, reduced to a cinder. According to one British officer, Henry Brackenbury, *'The town burnt furiously... blazed as though they had been ready prepared for the bonfire... Slowly huge dense columns of smoke curled up to the sky.'*

What of the people? What of those who lost more than their homes in the fire? And what is this slow ache in my chest I feel on reading this information?

In January 1981, a fire blazed through a flat in New Cross, where Yvonne Ruddock was celebrating her sixteenth birthday party. Thirteen people were killed, and another committed suicide two years later. Twenty-seven others were injured. In June 2017, a fire blazed through Grenfell Tower, a block of flats in West London. What started as a spark from an electrical fault spread due to wilful ignorance and lack of care from the local government.

In September 1985, Dorothy Groce was in her bed when police raided her home, looking for her son. She was shot, the bullet piercing her lung and exiting her body through her spine, causing paralysis from the waist down. Protests ensued, as a large group gathered outside her house, then moved to the local police station, demanding answers. When none came, the crowd grew angry and upset. They had nothing to lose. They were not being heard, and so violence grew, not from bloodlust, but from desperation.

In August 2011, when I learned that the catalyst for the riots was the murder of Mark Duggan, a Black man, a husband, a father, I was not surprised. Mark was subject to what is known as a hard stop: where three police cars surround and engulf with the intention to subsume those whom they suspect. A witness, watching the commotion from his ninth-floor flat, described the event as an execution: the carrying out of a death sentence on a condemned person. Wherever he had been, Mark Duggan did not have a chance; the sentence had been passed. Like a building damned, he had been marked for destruction. The *riots* which ensued followed a similar blueprint: a family searching for answers. No effort made by the police. Stories being read over. Erasure. Desperation. Necessity. Nothing to lose. Nothing to lose. Otherwise, what else is there to do but wait for the next time?

Maybe this is where I lose my faith, between the last disaster and the next. Maybe this is where I lose my faith: in the waiting.

*

After a preview screening of *Queen and Slim* at the BFI, I remained still in my seat, locked in stasis. I told my friend I didn't enjoy the film because I had spent two hours waiting for two Black people to die. I told him it hurt to watch because I spend much of my life waiting, waiting. I told him it hurt because, even knowing that this couple would die, the frame in which Slim holds Queen in his arms, both of them sprawled on the ground, both of them slain where they stood, surrounded by a wall of police, gutted me. I told him it hurt and he understood.

I came home from the cinema and my mother was on the phone to her best friend. I sent a greeting in Ga. *Miiŋa bo.* The women laughed. My mother said my Ga had come in a suitcase. We all laughed at this. I was saying the right thing, but I still sounded like a visitor in my own language. I speak Ga that has travelled. My Ga came in my mother's suitcase, when she arrived in London, in the early Eighties, and on pulling it out to wear, the garment had taken on a different quality. I speak Ga that has been warped and muted and emerged different; my Ga changed, long ago, when the British, hearing of the Portuguese success in a region of West Africa, then known as the Gold Coast, decided to join in the trade of Ghanaian gold and slaves. This is how I came to English: through an act of violence. I came to English by force. I came to English through British invasions and the sacking of towns and the burning of Kumasi.

I mourn the loss of my language and wonder what language there is for me to mourn in. What language could there be for such extraordinary grief? It is difficult to comprehend such loss when it goes unspoken, when it is suppressed and withheld and rendered silent. It is difficult to comprehend such loss when my languages have been warped and mutilated by violence.

I do not go back home. I haven't returned to Ghana in fifteen years. I couldn't return when my Grandma was being buried because my last connection there had been severed. I did not want to accept this. I do not go back home. I am not at home in Ghana. I call London home but I also know that this is not my home. I know I am, through the workings of various systems and institutions, not welcome here. This is not my home. I am not at home here or there. I am in limbo. I don't believe there is a word for this in Ga.

There is not a day in which I don't lose my faith in some way. There is not a day in which I am not mourning. There is not a day in which I do not believe. There is not a day in which I am not celebrating. There is not a day in which I am not tested. There is not a day in which I do not walk in my truth, yet know the way I am seen is a lie. I have lost my faith. I am losing my faith. I will lose my faith. I am stuck. I am in limbo. This existence becomes tiring. *Etomi.* I am tired.

To be Black is to be deliberate, lest you become spoken for. Your body is not yours; often, it is just a home for the fear of others. I come dressed for the cold and you still see danger in the shadows of my hood. I come to protest and you see a riot. I come with my hands up, and still you shoot. To be Black is to intend. It is to refuse. It is to lose your faith and still believe beyond the mourning. Otherwise, what else would we do but wait?

*

There is intention in expression. I shoot portraits on film, mostly of Black and Brown people. The last set I took were of my younger brother and sister, on a bright Christmas afternoon, where golden hour came down thick and heavy, the glow of a setting sun gorgeous and comforting and whole. There is a set of portraits I took on that day, one frame each, where for a moment, the limbo ceased. They were grounded. They were firm and sure and it was because they had surrendered. I asked them to step into this place of safety and they did so, on faith. They were both gazing towards the lens, something casting soft shadows across their faces, perhaps a fence. They held the gaze, staring towards the world in quiet defiance. I know they were both tired too, and that sometimes there are no words for what they can feel. And I know that these spaces are few and far between, but there was another frame where they are both laughing at something my sister said. Moving past pleasure, towards joy. Solace in expression. Intention, a language.

Language is the servant of meaning. Kamasi Washington said this, flexing broad fingers over a closed fist, this hand decorated by rings on each digit. When asked what kind of music he makes, he replied, 'Like most of the musicians around me, I'm making the art which is closest to the expression of who I am.'

There's an image which I've seen only once in person, but many times on a screen: *Five Men* by Roy DeCarava. He is described as a 'jazz photographer', as someone who might subscribe to the principle of spontaneous improvisation, as someone who might have wandered the streets of New York with quick feet and a sure heart, as someone who might have captured sounds to be seen, images to be listened to, voices to be felt; who might have encouraged us to feel the blues and jazz, the beat and bounce, the beauty, the ache, the joy. When I see this photo, of five Black men emerging from a memorial service held in Harlem for the children killed in the bombing of a church by white supremacists in Birmingham, Alabama, in 1963, I see what Roy might have seen, or rather, I feel that pull that he did, to pick up a camera, and let those in front of the lens know that they are seen. When I see this photo, I see one man with a direct gaze, another looking away, another looking down, another slightly obscured, another broaching the frame with the top of his head. Each figure is arresting in their gaze, or in their lack of one; each figure is mourning and celebratory; each figure is quietly defiant. Not silent, but quiet: full and present and in motion. Not being looked at, but *seen*, and allowing themselves to be so. It is difficult to comprehend this kind of loss, but in these moments, where one is not being suppressed and withheld and rendered silent, where one is allowed to express and grieve openly, it might begin to happen.

When I see this photo, I feel the pull from both sides. I am both image-maker and image. There is an exchange which takes place that escapes language but can be seen, can be heard, can be felt. I feel it. I feel it in that moment, when I have given the person on the other side of the lens a moment to breathe, a moment to be, just before I depress the shutter, when we are both whole and sure and grounded and gorgeous and defiant and free. I feel it. I feel it when the image emerges from development and the frame feels so rich and full, reflective of that aforementioned moment and everything which brought us to that brief infinity in which we could be anything, could be free.

When I see this photo, when I see my own, I understand that we all have our churches. We all have our places of surrender and solace; we all have our modes of defiance, we all have our modes of refusal, and I see how important it is that our sounds are seen, our images listened to, our voices felt.

*

These days, I spend my time using sentences like passageways, trying to build a small Church in which I can surrender. I am trying not to protect so much. I am trying to dream a little more. I am trying to find somewhere to house this ache, this beauty, this joy. I am trying to express, wholly, who I am. I am tired of waiting.

I think this is how I found myself in a living-room full of poets, a few days before Christmas, celebrating the holidays with jollof rice and drinks poured generously. Later in the evening, we clustered together in a loose circle, some seated, some standing, and reflected on the past year. We spoke of our visions for the future, near and far. We were saying things that were honest and true, God-like even. I would like to say that all our parents had come here from elsewhere, and if not our parents, then the generation before. I would like to say we are all tired of waiting. I would like to say we are all looking for our own language. Or, we are all looking for our own meaning, and trying to find the language that suits.

I've had the problem Solange Knowles described in an interlude on her album: the singular expression doesn't feel available. I used to think it was because I didn't know myself too well, but I'm wondering if there's too much for me to manifest in singular form; an enormous amount of matter has crushed into an infinitely small space. So I build churches in other places, where I can surrender. I build churches in other places to house my faith.

There is a place in south-east London, where, on a Wednesday evening, we converge to worship. We gather in quiet reverence, arriving early, waiting for friends to arrive. Perhaps a trip to the shop before we fill with conversation the void made by anticipation, waiting outdoors in the queue. During summer months, brown skin glowing in the lazy dusk,

the meeting of people you know, because this is south-east London, and
if we don't know you, we probably know someone who does, and if we
don't know someone who does, then perhaps, on laughing at that snip-
pet of conversation which spills from one exchange into our sphere, the
point pushed further, some more laughter, a back and forth, perhaps at
this point, there will be an introduction. We are gathered here for many
purposes, but one is shared by all of us: to breathe, to live, to be.

Inside, there is music. The voice of the MC introduces and hums, dances,
pierces, floats. There is a drum which knocks, knocks, knocks, inviting
you forward and back, forward and back. I find my faith somewhere in
the unknown, the unknowable, in the gap between the drums where
a trumpet might sneak through, towards me, towards us, a joyful horn,
a jubilant croon. I find my faith, gathered in a dark room under a set of
railway arches, in the calls and responses, the laughter, stepping with
strangers, in the frenzy of an extended solo, in the whoops and cheers,
in the joy of a collective dream of freedom. I find my faith here, where
I am mourning the wayward glance in my direction or the loss of life or
the incomprehensible grief, where I am mourning but I still believe. I still
believe there is more because, otherwise, what else is there to do but wait?

Afterwards we say things like 'I didn't know I needed that' or 'That was
a spiritual experience.' We follow each other into the night, beautiful
people splitting off at bus stops and train stations, waving goodbyes
through windows and ticket barriers, towards the safety of our homes,
touched, once more, by something larger than us, something divine.

INTERVIEW
SCHOLASTIQUE MUKASONGA

Scholastique Mukasonga is Rwanda's most celebrated author. Her eight works of memoir and fiction, all written in French, reckon with the country's tumultuous twentieth century in graceful prose distinguished by its warmth, directness and moral charisma. Combining the authority of traditional storytelling with the techniques of the social novel, her books explore themes of mourning and remembrance, female community, education and the insidious legacy of Rwanda's Christianisation. At their centre lies the struggle of Rwandan Tutsis, who suffered decades of violence and displacement before the genocide of 1994.

Born in 1956, Mukasonga spent most of her childhood in a resettlement village on Rwanda's outskirts, expelled with her family and thousands of other Tutsis by the independence era's Hutu nationalist government. She overcame poverty and strict ethnic quotas to attend college for social work, but fled the country in 1973, when Hutu classmates assaulted her and other Tutsis amid widespread killings. Mukasonga moved to Burundi and then Djibouti before settling in Normandy, where she was living when the genocide killed thirty-seven members of her family. She lost both of her parents and all but one of her siblings; their village was effectively wiped off the map.

Grief and the determination to rescue her loved ones from oblivion would inspire Mukasonga's first two memoirs, *Cockroaches* (2006) and *The Barefoot Woman* (2008). After their success, she began writing fiction, winning the Prix Renaudot for *Our Lady of the Nile* (2012). The novel brilliantly allegorises Rwanda's 1973 unrest – a harbinger of the genocide – through the intrigues of a Catholic girls' boarding school for daughters of the elite. An equally magnetic film adaptation by Atiq Rahimi debuted earlier this year.

Inspired by her mother's storytelling, Mukasonga's later fiction has turned decisively towards Rwanda's traditional culture, which she sees as a bulwark against racial division. The stories in *Ce que murmurent les collines* (What the Hills Murmur, 2014) reach back to the advent of colonialism and the collapse of Rwanda's ancient monarchy, while her most recent novel, *Kibogo est monté au ciel* (Kibogo Went Up to Heaven, 2020), features a rogue native priest defrocked for syncretising the gospels with the martyrdom of Kibogo, a local figure of legend. Mukasonga's latest work to appear in English is *Igifu* (2010), recently translated by Jordan Stump for Archipelago, a story collection that mixes autobiographical vignettes with moving portraits of Rwandan exiles in Burundi and France.

I met Mukasonga and her son Aurélien in May 2019 at the Freehand Hotel in Manhattan, where they were staying for the PEN World Voices Festival. A spirited conversationalist, she was disarmingly quick with her insights, quips and courtesies, such as telling me that I had 'the eyes of a calf' (in the traditional cow-centred culture of Rwandan Tutsis, a compliment). We subsequently corresponded over email during the summer of 2020; I have edited and translated our conversation from the original French.   JULIAN LUCAS

THE WHITE REVIEW You started your writing career in the genre of memoir, as a way, in your words, to 'answer the call of my dead'. But you have since written novels that explore Rwanda's history more expansively. How did grief lead you to a larger literary project?
SCHOLASTIQUE MUKASONGA I'm probably an atypical writer. I didn't have time to go looking for a model. I had an urgent duty of remembrance to perform, because I was living with the threat of losing that memory. I had to work with what I had, simply trusting in the blank page and making it my confidant. A confidant that welcomed my story without worrying about whether I'd written well or badly. When I started writing, in a little blue notebook that I always kept with me, I had no intention of publishing. I was saving memory. It was only after, through writing, I found enough respite to reflect, that I thought to share my story, to summon other guardians for it; and so, to publish.

My first two books, *Cockroaches* and *The Barefoot Woman*, are based on childhood memories of the Tutsi deportation camp in Nyamata, where I grew up. *The Barefoot Woman* is a tribute to my mother, and to all the courageous mothers forced, in those tragic years, to safeguard hope and to rescue their children. The books were paper graves that I had to build for my family, and for every victim who, lost in the genocide's anonymity, remains unburied. Because this grave had to be worthy of them, I was always concerned to write well. My father, who did not know French, demanded that his children speak 'a beautiful Kinyarwanda'. No doubt I inherited my care for language from him.

These first two memoirs were noticed by critics and received several awards, which encouraged me to persist in writing. Almost without noticing, I became an author. *Igifu*, my first short-story collection, was a transition to fiction. If some stories, such as 'Igifu' and 'Fear', are largely autobiographical, others, such as 'The Curse of Beauty', are more invented, while 'The Glorious Cow' draws on traditional Rwandan stories. Rather than a writer, I prefer to call myself a storyteller, as Rwandan mothers should be, because, as the saying goes, '*Umuntu uca umugani ntagira inabi ku mutim.*' The one who tells a story has no hatred in their heart.

TWR In 'The Curse of Beauty', my favourite story in *Igifu*, you seem to begin working more novelistically, weaving the story of a beautiful

Tutsi exile in Burundi into a larger allegory for the challenges faced by Rwandans at that time. What did longer fiction, and especially the novel, let you achieve that autobiography had not?
SM The novel gave me the distance necessary to widen my field of writing. It allowed me to approach themes such as the condition of women, traditions suppressed by missionaries, Rwanda's history and its racist falsification by Western anthropology. Novels liberated me, and if they remain, like my first books, a form of therapy, I've found pleasure in writing them, the same pleasure that my mother, Stéfania, must have felt in those evenings when she brought me and my sisters into the enchanted world of tales.

TWR Your first novel, *Our Lady of the Nile*, was adapted for film earlier this year. Could you describe your experience of the events that inspired the novel, and why you chose to retell them through the story of a girls' boarding school?
SM In 1973, when I was seventeen, Tutsi 'intellectuals', civil servants and students were expelled from their institutions. I had to go into exile and take refuge across the border in Burundi. At the time, I was only familiar with my village in Nyamata, my high school, Notre-Dame de Cîteaux [in Kigali], and the social-work school in Butare. My memories of Notre-Dame de Cîteaux, which was supposed to train the country's female elite, were the starting point for *Our Lady of the Nile*.

I wanted to take advantage of this new genre to rid myself of the poison that had ruined my adolescence, by inventing characters to whom I could lend some of my story. But I transposed them to an imaginary school, a microcosm of Rwanda in the 1960s and 1970s, when the country instituted a regime of ethnic apartheid and extended a Belgian colonial system that entrusted education exclusively to Catholic missionaries. [Belgium ruled the former German colony of Ruanda-Urundi under a 1922 mandate from the League of Nations.] This mass Christianisation profoundly uprooted Rwandan culture, causing the demonisation of ancient beliefs and the ostracisation of their guardians as sorcerers.

This is what I wanted to describe through the conflicts, hopes, illusions and despairs of the young girls in my novel, sequestered in their high school at an altitude of 2,500 metres during the rainy season that corresponds to a school year. I had no idea that I was obeying the old rules of seventeenth-century

French tragedy – unity of place, unity of time.

TWR Those who haven't read it might be surprised to learn that *Our Lady of the Nile* is, while certainly tragic, also extremely funny. What role does humour play in your work?

SM Humour, in Rwanda, is part of elegant social comportment. Rwandans wield it with great dexterity, even towards themselves, and even in the most tragic situations. Discretion, reserve and irony are characteristic of our culture. This can cause misunderstandings. To me, humour seems like the smartest way to convey a message, especially in a complex and painful story. This is what I've tried to do even in books like *Cockroaches*, written from pain. The distance that humour procures seemed necessary to me in the face of the genocide's unspeakability.

In a chapter of my latest book, *Kibogo est monté au ciel*, I introduce an eminent and sententious professor, who comes to Rwanda to demonstrate the existence of human sacrifices similar to those of the Mayas or the Aztecs in Latin America. It's a caricature – I obviously don't denounce the important contribution of the humanities – but how can we not be irritated to see our culture and our history interpreted according to Marxism, psychoanalysis, structuralism and other scientific modes? Kibogo may well punish the professor's arrogant science with his wrath.

TWR Rwanda seems to have had no shortage of dangerous outside interpreters, starting with the Catholic Church. In *Our Lady of the Nile*, the Mother Superior collaborates with the student zealots who want to track down their Tutsi class-mates. What's the connection between the Church and Rwanda's divisions?

SM Belgian colonists and Christian missionaries, mostly the White Fathers, considered Tutsis to be the only Rwandans capable of governing. Belgium imitated the British Empire's 'indirect rule', while the White Fathers dreamed of building a Christian kingdom in the heart of Africa. In the lead-up to independence, Rwanda had a short period of multi-party rule, but colonial and ecclesiastical authorities were concerned about the relationship between some Tutsi intellectuals and African progressive or revolutionary movements. It was the middle of the Cold War, and the Cubans were in Congo. Both Belgium and the Church turned coat and supported the Hutu party, the Parmehutu,

which had incorporated the racist ideology of 'foreign Tutsi' and 'indigenous Hutu'. We know what came next.

TWR Rwanda's old monarchy, which was abolished at independence, looms over the characters in *Our Lady of the Nile*. Virginia, your protagonist, ends up seeking the protection of an ancient queen's spirit. But I'd like to ask you about another royal connection, the one behind the novel's film adaptation.

SM I didn't expect *Our Lady of the Nile* to achieve such success. It was my first novel, an adventure. How far was that going to take me? And then, one day, I got a phone call from a Burundian friend. She told me that Charlotte Casiraghi, the daughter of Princess Caroline of Monaco and the granddaughter of Grace Kelly, had noticed my book and wanted to make a film. She asked to meet as soon as possible. The story of my book was becoming quite novelistic!

So I met Charlotte Casiraghi in April 2013. She told me that *Our Lady of the Nile* had come into her hands at a train-station bookstore in Lyon. 'I'd been intrigued by the name Scholastique,' she told me. 'I read it on the train and immediately thought it had everything necessary to make a beautiful film.' And she kept her word. She teamed up with her friend and producer Dimitri Rassam who, in the meantime – through the grace of Our Lady of the Nile – became her husband. The writer and director Atiq Rahimi agreed to shoot the film. I was thrilled by the decision. Atiq and I were friends. In 2008, I'd been invited to the Salon du Livre in Montréal as a guest of honour, and Atiq came as the winner of that year's Prix Goncourt. We met in pyjamas outside the Hilton, after the hotel was evacuated because of a small fire. He, the Afghan, and I, the Rwandan, rediscovered our refugee status in the Canadian night.

TWR How did it feel to see the story onscreen?

SM It made me cry. In the novel, I'd emphasised the force and dynamism of these young girls, who aren't adults, yet who find themselves cornered by adult divisions and hatreds. I had a little distance, because, though it isn't an autobiography, I had lived the experience at Notre-Dame de Cîteaux. But when I *saw* it, I couldn't move beyond the fact that these were, first of all, young girls, with all the dreams of young girls. You see to what extent Rwanda was enlisted in hatred and discrimination.

Poor Virginia and Veronica – and, yes, poor Gloriosa, who hunts her own classmates as I was hunted in Butare. [Virginia and Veronica are the school's only Tutsi girls. Gloriosa is the film's antagonist, a powerful Hutu minister's daughter who incites violence against them.]

TWR How closely involved were you in the film's production?
SM I had the official title of 'consultant'. Atiq Rahimi was anxious not to betray the book and to respect the complexity of Rwandan history and culture, quite far removed from that of Central Asia. The film was shot between March and December 2018. I was in Rwanda that September, and was able to assist Atiq, advising him to avoid certain anachronisms, as well as words and gestures that were contrary to Rwandan customs. I was very touched by his concern for authenticity.

TWR Did you know from the beginning that the film would be shot entirely in Rwanda?
SM Filming in Rwanda was imperative for me, but it was nevertheless an uncertain dream, completely dependent on budgetary decisions. Once I learned that this dream would be realised, I was determined to follow every step, whether on the spot in Rwanda or from France via WhatsApp. I can't imagine what the film would have looked like if the actresses hadn't been young Rwandans. Their accents – among the thousands of accents that prove La Francophonie is alive and well – are for me one of the charms of the film. Another is the beauty of Rwanda's landscape, which invites viewers to discover the country from a different perspective than that of the genocide.

TWR I was amazed to learn that the girls who played the students had never acted before, especially Amanda Mugabezaki, who portrayed Virginia.
SM Never. It's remarkable.

TWR How much did they know about the Rwanda where you grew up?
SM The young actresses come from the generation after the genocide. They had no direct experience of the era of anti-Tutsi discrimination. But they grew up with parents still living with its after-effects, which will take many generations to resolve. My mother told us stories about the kings of yesteryear, from her own time and others. The mothers of the

actresses in the film told their daughters the story of the genocide. The actress who plays Gloriosa [Albina Kirenga] told me that her parents were shocked when she told them that she was going to star in a movie. For a girl in Rwanda, where cinema is still in its infancy, it's an exceptional opportunity. But when the girl explained her role, her parents ordered her to quit or to risk being disowned by relatives who had survived the genocide. She took refuge with her grandmother, who also didn't approve, fearing that it would bring a terrible curse upon the family.

TWR Appearance and ideals of feminine beauty are central to your novel, and especially its conflict over who counts as a 'real Rwandan girl'. Gloriosa, for instance, condemns the boarding school's statue of the Virgin Mary for having an unacceptably narrow 'Tutsi nose'. Meanwhile, Fontenaille, the predatory old European, idolises Veronica for looking like an ancient Tutsi queen. How are these dynamics reflected in the film's casting?
SM At first, I thought we needed to find an ugly girl to play Gloriosa. I insisted. But my Gloriosa in the film couldn't be more beautiful. It's a lot subtler that way, and underlines that there were no true physical differences. They had to be simply young girls, all alike. The only one who's different is Veronica, so as to fit into the fantasy of Fontenaille, an old colonist who's fallen into decline and raves about saving the memory of the Tutsi. I knew a Fontenaille in Burundi, a completely decadent coffee planter. He even kept cows.

TWR Fontenaille is a terrifying character. He claims to adore the two Tutsi girls, but actually represents the beliefs responsible, historically, for their vulnerability. Could you explain the colonial origins of anti-Tutsi prejudice?
SM As I wrote in 'The Rukarara River' [published in *The White Review* No. 22], one of the greatest misfortunes to befall Rwandans, and especially the Tutsi, was to live near the sources of the Nile. The river's origin was a longstanding mystery, and in the second half of the nineteenth century, England's Royal Geographic Society organised expeditions to find it. In 1858, Richard Burton reached Lake Tanganyika, but it was his second-in-command, John Hanning Speke, who went on to Lake Victoria, concluding that it was the source of the Nile. Burton disputed his discovery, and in 1860, Speke embarked on a second

expedition to confirm it. He was fascinated by the political organisation of a region that would later be known as the African Great Lakes, where sovereign power rested on sophisticated rituals and court pageantry. Visiting a principality south of Lake Victoria, Speke informed the monarch that his 'race' was of Ethiopian origin, and had once practised Christianity. None of these explorers reached Rwanda, which they only knew from vague rumours. Yet before meeting a single Rwandan, they'd already sketched a forensic likeness, which under colonialism would harden into a mask. Tutsis were said to be tall, almost giants, with fine features, straight noses, and impassive bearing, of Caucasian type. They obviously came from elsewhere – possibly Ethiopia, but even further afield: Egypt, the Caucasuses, Tibet, the Ten Lost Tribes of Israel. Others savvily classed them as a race unto themselves: Hamites, descended from Ham or Cham according to the Bible. In any case, the Tutsi were evidently not Africans.

After colonisation, Europeans interpreted Rwanda's history in terms of races, invasion and feudalism. It was the birth of an ethnological myth, widely circulated in scholarly and missionary literature, that created a catastrophic division. Tutsis became strangers in their own country, aliens it was necessary to hunt or exterminate. There would be 'real Rwandans' – Hutus with a right to the land – and those not-at-home, the Tutsi. The Belgian creation of an ethnic identity card in 1931 would seal the division. Some Rwandan noblewomen succumbed to 'Egyptian fashion', wearing non-traditional hairstyles that evoked Queen Nefertiti. This flattering portrait did not erase the coloniser's suspicions. Beware the Tutsis' good manners and the fatal charm of their wives, said those who claimed to know us, for they are deceitful hypocrites. We know how such fantasies led to the genocide's abominable killings. Women and Tutsi girls were the first victims – raped, tortured, reduced to the condition of sex slaves. They were regarded by the *génocidaires* as tempting snakes, whose poisonous charm had insinuated itself among Europeans to slander and discredit the 'majority people' and conspire against their regime. Tutsi women and girls would pay dearly for the mirage of their beauty.

TWR As powerfully as you've written about the manipulation of feminine ideals, you've focused even more on communities of women, their

solidarity and resilience. What has this emphasis brought to your understanding of Rwandan history?
SM I've always loved to write about women in their everyday tasks at home or in the fields. In *Un si beau diplôme!* (Such a Beautiful Diploma, 2018) I describe my community of Rwandan exile girls in Gitega, Burundi. We lived in a dilapidated old colonial building, exchanging dreams of the future by the light of a hurricane lamp. In *The Barefoot Woman*, I describe the community of women that my mother wove around herself in Nyamata, a veritable parliament that met in our backyard. There, young girls learned good manners and the canons of Rwandan beauty, while advantageous marriages were arranged according to clan law. The women were the watchful guardians of tradition, sometimes going so far as to exile someone suspected of bringing bad luck to the village, but also ready to invent new rites to save a girl raped by militiamen from the anathema that weighs on child mothers.

TWR In Burundi, you were studying for a degree in social work, which you earned and later had to re-acquire in France. You haven't stopped practising the profession, even with all of your literary success. How does it inform your writing?
SM Becoming a social worker was without a doubt the only choice of my life. I believed that it would allow me to bring knowledge to those who had been excluded in the villages, to be their spokesperson with local authorities, and to extricate them from their marginalisation. Although I was unable to practise in Rwanda, in Burundi, I worked in rural areas with women who shared the same culture. In France, I fulfilled these same duties in a different context: to assert the rights of those at risk of being neglected, and to assist them in the improvement of their daily lives.

I've always said that being a social worker isn't just about giving. One receives much in return. When I first took on the heavy burden of being a survivor, I found comfort in a profession that always lets me feel useful to others, and in feeling that society expected me to be near those most in need. It gave me the strength to find peace and to write down my painful story. Writing, to me, also means lending my pen to those with no access to literature.

TWR Many of your characters go looking for the record of a past that has been kept from them. Prisca, in *Le Cœur tambour* (Drum Heart, 2016), reads about the nineteenth-century revolt of Queen Nyabinghi in a missionary's diary, which she discovers in an old church library. You've also discussed the neglect of Rwanda's oral traditions during your school years, when they were dismissed as 'backward' remnants of the old monarchy. Has rediscovering that archive been important for your writing?

SM When I was young, traditional storytellers and ritualists faced scorn and censorship from Rwandan politicians, but they attracted the interest of scholars, ethnologists and historians – both foreign and Rwandan – as the importance of safeguarding traditions and 'oral literature' became apparent. In a way, writing down this literature, hitherto transmitted by specialists of the royal court or storytellers like my mother, killed the freedom that had allowed storytellers to exercise their talent, and which made each telling unique. But at least it was preserved.

This rich literary harvest has remained beyond the reach of most Rwandans, even – or especially – those who entered the European school system. Many 'oral texts' only saw daylight in specialised journals with tiny audiences, which were quickly exhausted after their publication. These ethnographic collections were very difficult for ordinary Rwandans, even those who were literate, to access. The literature of Rwandan oral tradition was therefore reserved for ethnologists or Africanist historians. It remained a dead letter for the majority of young Rwandans educated in Europe. At Notre-Dame de Cîteaux in Kigali, my Kinyarwanda classes never addressed ancient literature. We never cared about studying *ibitekerezo*, historical narratives; *ibivugo*, heroic poems; *amazina y'inka*, pastoral poems; not even *imigani*, tales that could yet be heard at home. Our Kinyarwanda courses consisted of writing letters and administrative reports, or commenting on proverbs known to everyone. I've tried to catch up, often on the Internet, which offers many opportunities if you have the time and patience.

TWR When you grew up, French was the language of instruction in Rwandan schools. Since then, the government has promoted a shift toward English. What language, or languages, do you think will prevail in Rwanda's literary future?

SM Just as every individual counts, each language counts. Its value is not reducible to the number of its speakers. Any language, from the moment it allows an individual or a group of individuals to express themselves and thus to exist, ought to be preserved and considered among the riches of humanity.

Many Africans are fluent in three languages – their mother tongue, an African *lingua franca*, and a European language inherited from the colonial period. Rwandans have the inestimable treasure of sharing the same mother tongue: Kinyarwanda, which is the basis of education today. Swahili is the language of commerce, used throughout East Africa and much of the Democratic Republic of Congo. You will often hear it in Rwandan markets. French was imposed by Belgian colonists. (If the first great European war's outcome had been different, would I have spoken and written in German? I have often asked myself this useless question.) English arrived as a supplement, to expand the horizons of a small landlocked nation long reduced to a ghetto state by colonial and missionary rule.

Rwanda is now a member of the Commonwealth, while Louise Mushikiwabo, a former foreign minister, is Secretary General of La Francophonie. Future Rwandan literary talents will have the choice to express themselves in any one of these four languages.

TWR You have said elsewhere that writing in French might be 'temporary' for you. Would you ever write in Kinyarwanda?

SM For me, both languages are always present. In the 1960s and 1970s, French was taught in Rwandan primary schools. But it hardly left the classroom, because Rwanda was lucky enough to already have a national language spoken by everyone. So French, for me, was for a long time the language of writing. I wrote French before I spoke it, and even today, it seems to me that before I utter a French word, I have already written it in my head.

Besides, it seems to me that my 'beautiful Kinyarwanda' guides what I write even if, on the surface, French takes over. I often imagine that it's my mother who holds my pen or leans over my computer. French is not my mother tongue, but I think I've tamed it enough to make it tell Rwandan tales. The two languages share my thoughts and dreams: I don't know who operates the 'simultaneous translation'.

TWR Do you think you'll ever devote a book to contemporary Rwanda? Several of your memoirs conclude with glimpses of more recent travels home.

SM To write about the new Rwanda, I'd have to really settle there – not just what I do now, one month here, two months there. What truly interests me is the generation born after the genocide, who didn't know its brutality and have turned toward creation, autodidactically, especially in the countryside. Who don't necessarily want to leave the countryside, but to develop Rwanda so that it's not just Kigali, a 'Singapore', as foreigners have sometimes reproached. My project would be to write about an unencumbered Rwanda, because one doesn't want to be a hostage of history.

It's not that we're going to erase the years between the 1960s and 1994. But to build a house, you need a foundation. To build a solid Rwanda, one must go into the past, into the Rwanda of other times, which is why I wrote *Ce que murmurent les collines* and *Le Cœur tambour*. One reason I look to the past is because in that past, Rwandans lived together, without artificial differences, all children of the same father, Gihanga. [Gihanga is the legendary founder of Rwanda.] One looks towards that dignity of the past to build anew. So, I'm going to write about the new Rwanda – that's an obligation – but with a foundation in Rwandan tradition. Not in the void.

TWR Your story 'Death' from *Igifu* ends with a difficult return to Rwanda. The narrator is an exile, like you, and at the beginning we see her in France. Do you plan to write more about your adopted country, where you've lived for so many years?
SM I write about Rwanda, but I live in France. It's a bit like having two lives. My early life in Rwanda provided material for what I dare to call my auto-biographical trilogy: *Cockroaches*, *The Barefoot Woman* and *Un si beau diplôme!*. In the last of these, I devote several chapters to my move to France, the resumption of my studies to obtain a French diploma, my search for a job. But I am also present in my second country through the articles and columns I publish in newspapers. Of course, it is not impossible that I will one day dedicate a book to my professional experience in France. A social worker of African descent in the Norman *bocage* isn't so banal.

But I believe that I will never stop writing about Rwanda: there is so much more to write about this lost, murdered, recovering, reborn country. There are few Rwandan writers, and among them, even fewer women. I know my books are needed. It's as though I receive orders from young Rwandans who thirst to rediscover a culture so long obscured and despised. Writing to meet their expectations has become a duty, but also a pleasure. All I have to do is dig into the trunk of my mother's tales.

J. L.,
September 2020

HERVÉ GUIBERT

Shortly after the release of his 1990 novel *To the Friend Who Did Not Save My Life*, a poignant recounting of his battle with AIDS (recently republished in English by Semiotext(e)), Hervé Guibert announced his retirement. 'I don't see what else I could write,' the French aesthete, then visibly emaciated, told anchorman Bernard Pivot on the primetime literary programme *Apostrophes*. By this point, Guibert had already published some fifteen books, ranging from novels to essay collections and a photo-novel, most sitting uncomfortably between autobiography and fiction – making him a poster boy for the burgeoning trend of autofiction.

Born in 1955 to a middle-class family in the Parisian suburb of Saint-Cloud, Guibert spent his early years in the French capital before relocating to La Rochelle. His childhood was scored by the 'noise of sagging bodies' and 'skulls shattered on the tiles', heard during regular visits to slaughterhouses with his father, a veterinarian inspector. These morbid memories, starkly described in his early works, are typical of a macabre tendency – following in the tradition of French writers including Marquis de Sade and Jean Genet – which characterises much of his writing. Although his initial literary success was modest, the angelic-looking writer with the golden curls quickly became a fixture of the Parisian intelligentsia, striking up friendships with everyone from Michel Foucault to Mathieu Lindon and Sophie Calle, while making a living as a *pigiste* at *Le Monde*'s culture desk.

In the tradition of the *roman à clef, To the Friend* involves a constellation of real-life characters orbiting around its narrator – all renamed yet easily identifiable to a knowledgable reader. They include his long-time lover Thierry Journo and Journo's partner Christine Seemuller (who married Guibert in 1989 in order to become custodian of his estate) as well as public figures including Foucault, and Guibert's muse, the actor Isabelle Adjani. The controversial book brought Guibert fame. It also provoked national outrage, primarily in response to his thinly veiled chronicling of the death of Foucault, who appears under the moniker 'Muzil'. A friendship had grown between the men after a chance encounter at their local bakery in the 15th arrondissement of Paris in 1977, the year Guibert published his salacious debut novel, *Propaganda Death* (which caught the attention of the capital's queer literary circles, including his idol Roland Barthes). They sustained a longstanding camaraderie, punctuated with frequent dinner parties at the philosopher's apartment, predominantly attended by young writerly gay men. ('Why did you invite *her*?' Foucault once snapped at Edmund White after he'd brought Susan Sontag to one such gathering.)

We now know that Guibert eventually resumed writing, miraculously producing five more books and a film before his death following AIDS-related complications (exacerbated by a suicide attempt) in December 1991, soon after he turned thirty-six. As a critic, he wrote extensively about image-making, yet as a photographer, little was known about his work: only one catalogue of his images was published in his lifetime, based on an exhibition at Galerie Agathe Gaillard in 1984. This limited exposure is perhaps best explained by the fact that Guibert never truly considered himself a photographer. 'I take relatively few photographs, like an amateur,' he wrote, later evoking his admiration for two other self-proclaimed amateurs: Jacques-Henri Lartigue and André Kertész. This seems a wild understatement for someone who, over the course of two decades, took thousands of pictures: from self-portraits to thoughtfully choreographed portraits and still lives, mostly in black-and-white and taken with the small Rollei 35 his father gave him at the age of seventeen. Much like his writing, his photography features many loved ones: Journo, Adjani, his younger lover Vincent Marmousez and his beloved great-aunts Suzanne and Louise. Foucault was famously so fond of his portrait that he insisted it be used to accompany his biographies.

In *Ghost Image* (1981) – a book of essays written in response to Roland Barthes's *Camera Lucida* (1980) – Guibert wrote that he most enjoyed photographs that are blurry, poorly framed, even those taken by children – marked by flaws, resisting a sense of reality. This is perhaps where photography and writing meet in Guibert's oeuvre: they are technologies of the self through which the manipulation of the real becomes possible. It took nearly twenty years and a posthumous retrospective at Paris's Maison Européenne de la Photographie in 2011 for Guibert's photographic work to receive institutional recognition. Today, it is widely celebrated for its intricate subjects, delicate compositions and evocative, often carnal storytelling.

BENOÎT LOISEAU

This is an extract from a longer essay on Guibert's work, which can be read in full on The White Review's *website.*

PLATES

I	*Michel Foucault*, 1981
II	*Le Table de Travail*, 1989
III	*New York*, 1981
IV	*Sienne*, 1979
V	*Thierry Do*, n.d.
VI	*Santa Caterina, panier de fraises*, 1990
VII	*Autoportrait avec Suzanne et Louise*, 1979
VIII	*Isabelle*, 1980
IX	*Autoportrait*, 1989
X	*Vincent couché*, 1988
XI	*Le Fiancé III*, n.d.
XII	*Musée non identifié*, 1978
XIII	*Grille T. (de près) S.C.*, 1982
XIV	*Thierry Toilette dans la sacristie*, 1983
XV	*Les billes*, 1983

I

IV

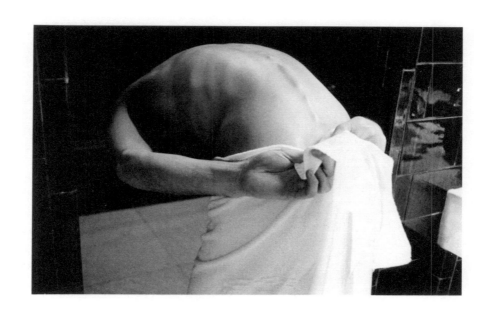

VI

VII

XII

XIII

XIV

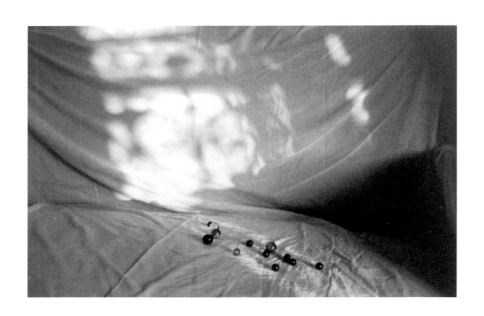

BOYS
BRANDON TAYLOR

Carson worked open to close at the deli. He sliced the ham and turkey and laid it out on a bed of spritzed lettuce. He baked the wings, and pulled them, still sizzling on the pan, from the oven. Then, twelve at a time, he glazed them in sweet chili or barbeque or buffalo sauce, portioning them into their containers with the chopped celery and goopy ranch dressing. These he stocked in the front of the case for the grab-and-go. And then it was the usual sandwiches: turkey club, spicy wrap, T, chicken breast, ham and swiss. This was all easy enough, simple, direct work that he could do without thinking. He liked the peace of the grocery store before it opened and before the cooks at the hot station started their prep which entailed a lot of clanging metal implements and blasting world music at full volume from their phones. He liked when it was just the blue-grey of the lights on low and the hum of the freezers.

Right before the grocery store opened, and that first flood of people came in, anxious and bleary-eyed, Carson took out the boxes he had opened. He dropped them, flattened, into the dumpster, kicked over a crate and smoked two cigarettes, one after the other.

The morning was summer-cool, but growing hotter each minute as the sun spread across the parking lot like a slowly opening eye. Soon, he'd be in the middle of it, but for now, he was in the safety of its eyelid, smoking and watching gnats mass and disperse over the rotting fruit out back.

He sometimes thought that his life had gone horribly awry and he sometimes thought that working in a deli grocery was exactly what he could have expected from this world. His mother had worked in a factory, and his father had not worked at all. He came from good and ordinary people for whom any paycheck at all was a miracle. Carson's great misfortune was that he had believed, if only for a short time, in the delusions of his education. His mind and sense of self had been meddled with, but now, at thirty-one, he had shed the idea that he would do great and wonderful things in the world. He had outgrown it, slipped free of its constraints.

He flicked his cigarette up and away, and it spun like a paper football until it landed in a divot in the pavement.

*

Around noon, Carson was re-cutting turkey breast for the front cooler. Teddy, one of his co-workers, was in the back too. He'd been to another high school baseball practice over the weekend and had the sunburn to prove it.

'How do you even know that these things are happening?' Carson asked.

Teddy looked up at him, confused at the question. 'The team manager told me.'

'The team manager of a high school team? Told *you* that they'd be practising?'

'I gave him twenty bucks,' Teddy said, like that made it clear. But Carson had learned not to question Teddy's methods, nor his motivations for spending three to four hours in the sun watching shirtless high school boys fling balls at one another as hard as they could. Teddy had invited Carson to watch with him, and Carson had said that he'd think about it. The idea of going out to the edge of town and sitting on the back of Teddy's truck, drinking cold beer and sweating, trying to fit in with the other people, the parents and the siblings and whoever else had come along to watch, as though they had a right to be there, too, seemed exhausting in a way that he could not explain without insulting Teddy.

'Sure, alright,' Carson said. Teddy had hooked a Bluetooth speaker to his phone. He played 'The Boys are Back in Town' and that 'Bad Boys' song from *Cops*, which had always struck Carson as somewhat ridiculous. That a show about the police dragging anonymous people from their cars and their homes had a theme song sung by a black reggae artist. It seemed to him either thoughtless or ironic in the way that white people conceived of irony, when there was someone else's neck exposed. But Teddy played those songs and songs like them on a loop while he loaded and unloaded the dishes.

The meat was cold, and Carson's fingers grew bloodless and white. His knuckles hurt from holding the knob while he glided the breast back and forth over the sharp blade, cutting it into thin sheets that he carefully laid across each other in delicate layers, a lattice of translucent white flesh.

When he was done, he took the platter back out front and put it into the cooler from the back, sliding the empty platter out and balancing it on his knee so he could pull the cooler door shut.

Roma was making a turkey club to order. She held the panini machine closed over the sandwich like it had wronged her. She raised her chin at Carson, and he raised his chin at her, laughing.

'These people,' she said.

'That bad, huh?'

'This is my fifteenth sandwich in ten minutes. There must be some kind of field trip happening,' she said.

Roma was twenty-four, and had graduated just a few weeks before with a degree in political science. She had the weary affect of someone who had read a lot of theory but viewed herself as distinctly different in character from the other people who had read a lot of theory because she had *self-awareness*. And it was true, she was self-aware, to a point, though sometimes all the things she knew about the rise and corruption of power and the way the American political apparatus functioned would flare up with all the awkward, nervy energy of someone going to their first sleepover without parental supervision. Which was to say that she had a lot of principles and a lot of ideas, but no real outlet for them.

She made the sandwiches in the deli because she liked being able to call upon a predetermined set of steps and instructions. Carson had felt the same way when he was new. There was less chance of a mistake when you knew all the steps required for a ham and swiss or a turkey club or a T or a chicken salad sandwich. Even when people got very *particular* about not wanting tomato or wanting red onion or wanting this specific kind of spread, there were really only so many combinations of things, only so many sandwiches under the heavens.

But it was the summer, and sometimes there were field trips or day camps or things like that, the odd flurry of activity that meant sandwich after sandwich after sandwich, each one the same or a little different from the one before, and it was possible in the daze of nudging the bread onto the metal counter and cutting it this way and that, spreading the mayo or the southwest sauce on it and assembling the meat and vegetables, to glimpse the whole of your life as a series of sandwiches made and handed over the counter to strangers you would never see again. And it was on those days that life in the deli was a little stranger and a little sadder and a little smaller than it seemed to be otherwise.

'Hang in there,' Carson said, and Roma rolled her eyes and sighed dramatically. She mimed a noose and let her head go slack.

'Hang *me*,' she said, then laughed.

Carson paused with his hand on the swinging doors. Roma was shorter than him, quite pale with dark brown eyes. She was wearing a baseball cap to keep her hair out of her face. She stood with her hands in gloves, hip cocked to one side, pressed against the counter on which the panini machine rested, heating the sandwich. She had a fleshy but athletic build, and did not seem like the sort of person who might casually make a lynching joke to a black person, but here she was doing it.

She seemed to understand after a moment or two of silence, but by then Carson was pushing on the door in earnest and leaving through it.

He felt embarrassed for her more than offended. Because he knew that she'd hate herself a little for having done it, and he'd have to endure an embarrassed apology text message in the next day or so.

The real hazard of working and living with white people, Carson felt, was not that they did the racist thing exactly. It was having to attend to all of the fall-out of the racism. Their embarrassment. Their pity. Their self-flagellation. All their white apologies. Their apologies about their apologies. Their liberal intelligence. Their moral schemas. All of their theory. The Derrida. The DiAngelo. The Foucault. The Baldwin. The Crenshaw. The conservation of violence. The smarter white people were in general, the worse their apologies turned out. Like some kind of weird, multi-armed liberal blob.

When he was growing up, Carson had dealt with real racism. A white man had once spat at his grandmother outside of a Dollar General. He had been called a nigger on the school bus every single day of kindergarten by wide-eyed white children. He had seen Confederate flags flying from the backs of trucks as the seniors pulled out of the parking lot in high school. Once, in middle school, a girl who had been his friend had called him a nigger to her friends at break because he'd outscored her by three points on a physical science test. Each of those moments had been awful, but somehow bearable, because he hadn't also had to deal with the collective mass of white guilt that came attached to it. The racists in Alabama had just been racist. They knew who they were and what they were about. They didn't go around trying to make you feel sorry for their moral depravity. They didn't see it as a moral failing.

And yes, if pressed, Carson certainly would choose liberal racism over the usual racism, but there was something also particularly draining about liberal racism. And what he thought was the real work of racism was the fact that somehow people presented this choice to him like it didn't represent the problem itself. The fact of racism. Its pervasiveness, like the capitalism the white people he slept with were always complaining about.

When he sat down on the folding chair in the back next to Teddy, he was not surprised to see a text from Roma already – *Can we talk? I'm so sorry.*

The sad and predictable nature of it was what bothered him most.

*

At around five, a fireman that Carson sometimes fucked came into the deli section looking for dinner.

He was tall and broad, roasted a dark red colour, and he had a network of poorly inked tattoos tangled down his right arm ending just above the elbow so it could be hidden behind his shirt. Carson recognised him immediately, even before he came fully into view, by the cant of his body, that weird, slightly forward-leaning walk of his. The odd hitch in his step from a hip injury three years ago. He had a thick neck and his head sat quite low.

When he saw Carson, he did a double-take, then came over.

There were two varieties of straight men who also fucked men. The kind who avoided you in public for fear of being found out. And the kind who treated you like you were in the same frat, a giddy kind of comradery.

'Look who's here,' Marat said.

Carson rested his elbows on the top of the cooler even though they weren't supposed to. He drummed his fingers against the glass and watched as Marat's eyes travelled all over him. His body warmed to the idea of the two of them slipping out and finding some discreet, dark place.

'Here I am,' Carson said.

Marat laughed and stuck his thumb through the loop of his belt. His suspenders pulled tight down his shoulders and chest. He had a bit of a belly, but it was hard with muscle. He wasn't defined. Not really. Just pure bulk. Pure man.

'Haven't seen you in a while. Where you been hiding?' Marat squatted, rooted through the plastic containers of the prepackaged meals of wings and the half chicken breast with potato and the chicken parm on gooey noodles.

'Nowhere,' Carson said. 'I've been around.'

Marat stood and tucked two containers of sweet chili chicken wings under his arm. He squinted playfully like he didn't believe Carson. The last time they had slept together was about three weeks before when they went up to Lake

Macbride and swam and drank all day. Then, the sun dropping below the horizon, they undid their swimming shorts in the bed of Marat's truck and lay down on their damp blankets. Carson's skin was sensitive from the sun, and Marat's chest hair scraped him raw. But it was an exhilarating hurt, the kind that was the best companion to pleasure. When they were done, they sat on the tailgate and drank the last of the beer from the cooler. They were at the edge of a country road, trees all around them, everything smelling like cedar and pine and summer grass. Everything itchy and hazy with pollen and dust. The sky overhead purple and rich and full of light. It was one of those perfect summer evenings, and Carson lay back and closed his eyes, and he must have stayed that way a while because the next thing he remembered was a cop shining a flashlight into his face and kicking the tyres on Marat's truck. Telling them to leave. His stomach jumped, and his mouth went dry. A flicker of panic when he saw their faces behind the beam, because there he was, wet and shirtless in the back of a truck, caught out. But Marat was already in the cab, laughing with one of the troopers. Saying that they were just sleeping off the drink and would be on their way in a minute or two. The cop who had his light trained on Carson's face, that too-brilliant beam of light that burned its way into his brain and made his teeth hurt, smirked. He slapped the side of the truck.

Marat had his arm out of the window, gesturing while he talked, like it was nothing. That easy, common way white men had of talking to other white men, thinking nothing of what might become of them both. Carson tied the drawstring of his shorts, and secured the bucket of empties under the storage chest. Then he climbed over and hopped down into the dry grass. The cop stood there, his thumbs in his waistband, hand close to his firearm. He had a thick, sunburned neck, and blood-shot eyes.

'Excuse me,' Carson said, but the man didn't move. He stood there a moment longer. Right in Carson's way, like he was daring Carson to brush him as he went by. But Carson stood, the grass so itchy against his ankles, holding his breath. He watched the cop run his tongue around his teeth, the bulge in his lip and cheek. Marat's hoarse, dry laugh from the cab of the truck as he said, 'Come on, skip.'

Carson said nothing in return to that. He waited for the cop to move. And eventually the cop took a step back, permitting just enough space for Carson to go by him. Carson squeezed through that space and when his hand was on the door latch, the cop said, 'You can't say excuse me?'

There was another beat of silence then. And the distant sound of the other people leaving Lake MacBride on the main road. The cop talking to Marat leaned down and squinted through the cab to see what was happening, and Carson's eyes met Marat's. Then, a slow, subtle shake of Marat's head in the shadow of the truck. Carson breathed out.

'Excuse me,' he said. He could feel the cop smile. He did not have to see it to know. The cop behind him laughed and the other one laughed too and they walked off after slamming the tailgate shut behind them. The force of it made the truck shake and shift. Carson tried very hard not to jump when the noise of it fell over them.

When they were on their way, Marat reached through the dark of the cab and touched Carson's neck where he was still tingly and raw, and Carson moved away from him. The drive was quiet. They didn't play the radio or stop to use the bathroom, though they both had to go. They didn't stop until they were back in Iowa City, and Marat dropped Carson at home, and Carson went inside and felt, for the first time since the cops had woken him, that he could breathe freely.

When he tried to sleep, he kept thinking about Marat's laughter with the cops. How they acted like they knew each other, and perhaps they did. Perhaps they all did. All the cops and firemen in the world one laughing cohort. All of them joined in fraternity. Us and them. Those who know and those who don't. Brothers, Carson thought. They were all brothers. But he couldn't sleep. Not that night and not the next. He just kept hearing their laughter.

In the deli, Marat said, 'I feel like you been avoiding me.'

'Nah,' Carson said. 'I haven't been.'

'I texted.'

'It's been busy,' Carson said. 'It's been a busy summer. I work open to close.'

'All the time?'

'Don't you put out fires all the time? People gotta eat.'

Marat laughed. That same laugh, which in the chill of the deli made Carson shiver.

'Let's hang out soon,' Marat said.

'Bet,' Carson said, patting the top of the counter.

Marat hesitated a moment longer, seemed to be on the edge of saying something. But didn't. He turned and went away with his dinner, and Carson watched his broad back retreat.

Overhead, the grocery store music changed from Bon Jovi to John Cougar Mellencamp.

*

It was the last hour of Carson's shift, which meant breaking down boxes and carrying them out back. He wiped down all the counters, checked the dishwasher one last time. They weren't allowed to store things in it overnight. But he could take the last load out when it was still warm and put it away on the racks and shelves. The measuring implements and knives burned his hands when he removed them, but by the last row, he had no sensation left and could do it more easily. He mopped the back room after the boxes were broken down and stashed near the door so he could take them out when he left. He turned out the light, the floors still slick and smelling like lemon cleaner. Then the spritzing of the front cooler, wiping it down too, making the glass shine. The machines he scraped and cleaned. They would have to be disassembled in a couple of weeks for a more thorough job, but for now, they just got the usual soap and rinse.

He turned out the light in the cooler and watched it go dark. Then the rest of the deli. Everything in its place. Everything clean and bright. Everything settling down to sleep. He carried the boxes tucked up under his arm and hefted them over into the dumpster. He stood in the empty lot, watching the other grocery store workers empty out and get into their cars.

On the other side, he could hear the musicians still playing in the Ped Mall. Country and folk covers. There was a black guy with heavily relaxed hair who wore a headband and sang the strangest covers of Michael Jackson that Carson had ever heard. People danced while the fountain sputtered up into the air behind them. They shimmied and rocked, their elbows tight to their bodies and their knees locked. They moved as if they were trying to gingerly make their way across a thin sheet of ice, like their weight would cause the ground to shear open. Like watching one of those wooden toys at a flea market jerk to life when you turned a wheel. They danced and laughed and clapped at the end of each song, and another one started up. Purple and pink and blue lights flickered through the night as the little show sputtered through its sequence.

Carson walked along the edge of the crowd, near the playground, watching as people enjoyed themselves, seemed to really abandon themselves to the pleasure of the moment. Further back into the Ped Mall, the bars were full, their doors flung open, pumping their music into the air too, creating a hash of genres and sounds.

He passed under the trees downtown, and the people having their dinners out on the raised wooden platforms, servers darting in and out to lay plates or pick up finished dishes. They poured water from sweating carafes and swatted at mosquitos. The Old Capitol shopping centre sat impassively on the other side of the street, its signage dim and pulsing blue and white. People walking there too, so many people out this weekend at this hour.

Carson crossed the street and dipped down towards the river. He crossed near the union and kept going, over the bridge and up the long hill by the Art Building, that silver metal monstrosity. He lived near some of the frats, which sat on a hillside and overlooked the campus and Hancher. They were old, kind of charming brick buildings, not entirely out of place among the low-rent duplexes and apartment buildings strung out to the East and North. The other frats were back across the river, and fanning out along the edge of town, shrouded in trees.

Carson had been in Iowa for a few years now. He had come down from Wisconsin with a woman he was seeing when she'd relocated for a job in the creative writing department. The job had made her miserable and unhappy. She had taken to blogging, and by accident he'd discovered a few articles she had written for a digital magazine about the inequality in their relationship and how she felt as a white woman with a black boyfriend who made less money than she did and who had not gone to college. It had been an ugly way to discover what she thought of him, but in the end, he had been grateful for it, because it was a rare thing to find out the unvarnished truth of what someone felt for you or did not feel for you, as it were. He packed up his things and got a job at the deli, and a couple of months later she was attacked online for *white feminism* in her collection of essays for which she had been paid $500,000.

It wasn't true that Carson had not gone to college. He had gone to State for a year and a half before it had gotten to be too expensive and too hard. Then he had left to go and stay with a buddy in Wisconsin, sleeping on his couch and working at a restaurant out by Lake Monona. That was how he had gotten involved with the woman essayist. She came in after workshops on Tuesdays and after her classes let out on Thursday nights, with two of her friends, a poet and an anxious fiction writer who was, he said, working on a novel made up of a series of comic vignettes. They ate oysters and drank rosé, and when it was time for entrées, they split large dishes. After the third week of that, Carson asked her out, and she said yes, and they went out to see the fireworks over the lake and then ate ice cream on the union steps. Then, in the doorway of her apartment, she gripped his cheeks and said, with a glossy, luminescent buzz going, that she wanted him to eat her out until she said he could stop. And so he did. And then they were dating.

The woman essayist liked a lot of things. She liked to be called bitch when they were having sex. And she would work herself up into a panting, quivering state that had not so much to do with him as what was unfolding behind her eyelids, and she'd ask him to finish inside of her and then seem to change her mind at the last minute and ask for it on her stomach, no on her face, no, in her mouth, no inside of her. And what he learned after she changed her mind the third time was that she wanted him to keep going, that what she sought was the friction, the tension between her professed desire and his unwillingness to give it to her. And afterwards, when he asked if she was okay, she just laughed and offered him tissues and said that she was great, fine, that she'd be alright, and she lay back and finished herself.

They ate spaghetti dinners with sauce that Carson made. He'd spend hours on a Saturday night making marinara and freezing it into cubes so that he could have fast, quick dinners. Before her workshops, when her work was to be discussed, she was impossible to live with, so Carson slept at his buddy's place. *I'm just really trying to refine this idea* was what she said most often, sitting at her desk, shoulders square to the task before her. Sometimes she'd look at him and Carson felt completely transparent, like she was picking over what was inside of him and discarding what she didn't need.

The other people in her programme did not like her very much. They sometimes said that she was selfish. What amazed Carson was that they would sidle up to him at a party or a bar, and they'd lean in and breathe wet, cold air on his face, their lips frothy with foam. And they'd say, *She treats you like shit, man.* And, *She's got no right.* And, *She's a monster.* Carson patted their cheeks. Sometimes, he kissed them when they said this. Sometimes, he rubbed their heads like they were docile, silly pets. Because it was true that she gave herself over to her work, that she was burning herself up from the inside out. But it was her work. It was her life's purpose. He didn't have any right to say how she should pursue it. He was drawn to her because he didn't have a calling in life, and he found her fascinating.

But what he understood later, when he read her blog, was that she had been using him all along. She hadn't kept him from reading her work out of a sense of self-preservation. She hadn't avoided it out of shyness. She had been taking from him. All the stories he'd told her about his grandpa and the farm. The cold, dark winter. The way no one in his family had really spoken to him as a child. The way men had climbed on top of him as a boy. The way they'd shot and killed deer to have something to eat. The way the roaches climbed out of his backpack at school. All of that. He'd told her in bed while they lay together, breathing and feeling close to one another. He had told her, and she had taken without asking. Folded it into her *analysis* of a working-class ethic. She'd turned his past into a story. What could you say to someone who did that?

Carson sometimes felt that he drifted through the world, a man without a country to which he could return, because she'd stolen from him so thoroughly, so rigorously. She'd left the bone of the past completely clean. What did he have left for himself? He understood, by degrees and then all at once, that what he'd thought of as a kind of mutual affection and care and desire had really been greed on her part. She'd been *fascinated* and had used him. And it was true, Carson knew, that people used each other. He certainly used people. That's how you got by in the world. Using and taking. But also giving. But also sharing. But also caring. But also, also, also.

In the backyard of his building, Carson opened another cold beer and relaxed into the chair. The boys in the frats were grilling up the street, and the smell of their food drifted down to him. That and the sound of their music. Their laughter. Women's voices rising, too, among all the shouting men. Rectangles of light dropped down from the apartments above him, landing on the grass to his left and to his right. He had a little smoke going to keep the gnats and mosquitos away.

His back hurt in a vague, distant way when he shifted too sharply or abruptly. His fingernails were white and stiff from so much cleaning all day. Washing his hands every five minutes, it seemed.

His phone was mute on his lap, and he considered texting Marat to see where he was and what he was doing. He could make out the whine of a siren if he tried. It was the side of the river with the hospital and all night he could hear sirens and helicopter blades as people worse off than he was were brought in and taken care of. Some of them lived. Some of them died. Some of them went on in the grey in-between as their families gathered and waited and prayed and hoped and breathed. That was all of human tragedy. Grey waiting.

He lit a cigarette, and as if drawn from the great expanse of the world, a text message from Marat landed on his screen.

Hey

Carson imagined his split nails and stubby fingers tapping out those three letters in his narrow bed across town. Next to his girlfriend or whatever she was. Carson texted *hey* and put his phone face down on his stomach. He closed his eyes and let the cigarette smoke drift overhead and away.

Below him, the lamplights lining the lakeshore path. Hancher's golden glow. The glinting landscape of downtown, beautiful at this distance and hour. It seemed so much grander than it was, like if you added it all up it might surprise you even if you knew the sum already, like some final, magical trick to the arithmetic would show itself.

Marat texted back that he was in Carson's part of town and could he come over, and Carson said sure, okay, he was in the back. It was fifteen, then twenty minutes later when Marat came around the building. They were in the shadow of trees and the complex. The whirr of the units and the ventilation filled the air. The heat of the day had broken into something bearable. The night was cool. Clear.

'Twice in one day,' Carson said. 'To what do I owe the honour?' He raised his bottle. Marat lowered two bottles wrapped in cold towels to the grass and popped the top on one. They clinked the base of the bottles, like they did in Barcelona, something Carson had picked up in Wisconsin.

Marat's chair sank into the grass, and seemed to want to give out under his weight. He exuded a dense, animal heat. He had a baseball cap turned backwards and wore a sleeveless jersey. He smelled *clean*. Like soap. He seemed to regard the smoke drifting out of the device at Carson's feet with suspicion. Like it would leave him smelling bad.

'You off to Saloon?'

'Might hit up Studio,' Marat said.

'Living dangerously,' Carson said. Studio was the gay bar. A little carve-out in an alleyway near a bank. The first time Carson had gone there, he'd walked by it five times before he saw someone disappear under a pull-down door. Inside, it had been mist machines and pulsing music, so clichéd he'd wanted to leave, but had not.

'Looking for something particular,' Marat said.

'Cheers to that.'

Marat rolled the bottle between his hands. Didn't drink. Carson leaned back in his chair and shut his eyes again.

'You'd tell me if we weren't alright, yeah?'

'I'd tell you.'

'I been feeling like it's funny between us. I don't know why. Since that night. At the lake.'

'I don't know what to tell you about that. Been working. You too, I assume.'

'Yeah, I been working too. But still.'

Carson sat forward on the chair and set his bottle down into the grass, but held the lip of it with his finger to keep it upright. He looked down into the dark between his legs and not at Marat. But he could feel Marat looking at him, waiting, silent.

'What do you make of that, up at the lake?' Carson asked.

'Not sure what you mean.'

'Up there, with those two cops. What do you make of that?'

'The boys? Oh please. They were just giving us a hard time. I imagine they see that shit two, three times a day. Bored, most likely.'

'It didn't feel like boredom,' Carson said.

'I knew it was something. I could feel it.'

'I'm not saying it's *something*. I'm just asking what you made of it.'

'They weren't going to do anything. Not to you, anyway. Not with me there.'

'What if you hadn't been there?'

'Everything ain't about that, Carson. I thought you knew that.'

Carson felt his face grow hot. Not in shame or embarrassment. But anger. The nape of his neck tingled. Marat reached out and put a hand on Carson's knee, and Carson wanted to crack his head with the bottle. He picked it up by the neck, squeezed tight. Considered it. Saw in the purple-black of the night air a glittering, silver premonition of what might happen if he did.

'It's always about that for me,' Carson said. 'I don't get a choice.'

'Come on, man,' Marat said.

It was a thing that people did. Expect forgiveness without ever having to say that they were sorry or that they had done anything wrong. It was the other kind of white apology. The more selfish kind because it concealed even as it took, made invisible the thing that had made the apology necessary in the first place.

Carson closed his eyes.

'Bearing with one another and, if one has a complaint against another,' he said, drawing the verse up from memory, all those Sundays, all those years of belief before it had turned cold and dark. What he had left were verses and sayings. Residue at the bottom of the cup of belief. Silty remnants. 'Forgiving each other. As the Lord has forgiven you, so you also must forgive.'

'What kind of mumbo-jumbo is that?' Marat asked.

Carson regretted having left the South for this heathen North. Where no one believed in anything and everyone thought they had to abide by certain common rules. What they believed in was the law. What was legal and illegal. They thought not of what they did to each other except as it pertained to the legal code. Not what they did to other people.

'That is the law of man,' Carson said. 'The law of God.'

'I didn't know you were a Christian type,' Marat said.

'I'm not. I was. But I'm not. Anyway, don't worry about it.'

'You say don't worry about it. You didn't say shit about being upset before.

But now you're treating me like I'm your enemy. How am I your enemy?'

'I didn't say that.'

'You want to change the story so bad. You want to make it about that. It's not about that.'

'About what? Can you even say it?'

'Nobody called you a nigger,' Marat said. 'Nobody did anything to you.' He stood up, loomed over Carson. The music from up the street was louder. The frat boys shouting. Marat bent down and put his hands on both the chair arms. Tilted Carson back. Carson saw his red face. The veil of the trees overhead. The stars.

'You're angry because I made you think about it,' Carson said. 'You're angry because I made you think about something that's hard and that you're neck-deep in.'

'I'm not neck-deep in anything,' Marat said. 'I didn't do anything. I'm clean.'

'Nobody's clean,' Carson said. 'That's the thing. Nobody's free of it. We're all in it all the time.'

'You're being so fucking strange. Are you on something?'

Carson pushed his weight down and felt the chair slip free of Marat's hold. Marat shook his head and sat down too. Scooted his chair over.

'I keep going over it in my mind. I keep running it back. And I keep hearing you laugh. I can't get it out of my head. You laughed.'

'Was I supposed to do something else? Make a scene? March in the streets?'

'No,' Carson said. 'It's that you laughed. It wouldn't have occurred to me to laugh.'

'It was just harmless shit, Carson. You're making too much of it.'

Carson nodded. He pushed up from the chair and handed Marat his beer.

'Maybe,' he said. 'I might be.'

'Where you going?'

'To bed,' Carson said. 'You have your hunting to do.'

'I came to make it right between us.'

'We're alright.'

'It doesn't feel alright.'

Carson laughed then, put his shoulders back and laughed for all he was worth. And when he was done, when his chest and stomach hurt from laughing, when his eyes were wet with tears, and his throat was raw, when he was all laughed out, he turned to Marat and said, 'It never does.'

LAURA ELLIOTT

POETRY

MONUMENT IV

Either way artefact
take me
with a part smile and
a broken arm,
I am on for
a famous adventure.

Perfectly warm potential,
the monument slips
masterpiece
into the conversation -
a bitter
pig cheek.

What is she thinking,
monument,
dressing in
her marrow, flaking
into the wet sauce
of our least agreement.

Might still have
forty-five minutes,
might only have
forty-five years.
Come on then, monument -
with your tart

borrowed friendships
and multiple towels
for the week,
show me which
way round you
want me.

MONUMENT V

More physical technologies
of memory, more ways

to uproot the sentimental
routine, wiring feeling

through the woody core.
Wring my monument out

she is sodden with grief,
clothes so heavy

she cannot walk
and I cannot carry her

around this mossy city.
I need a machine

to winch her
from the iron pedestal,

I need her to come with me
or I won't remember.

Tender nursery, she is patient
with my attention,

makes me whisper -
monument, oh

my monument,
monument.

MONUMENT X

Refraction
never hurt
anyone –

look at some
paintings
again

they are not
monuments
but you can

use them
to measure
the cruelty –

how well will
she fracture
how well can

you slice off
a portion –
brick red apple

lamentable
flayed marble –
build up a

picture make
it sufferable.

MONUMENT XI

Ideal monument carriers
include birds or pigs

or wolves or bears
or rushes or laurel

or holly or briars
or apples or grapes

or lemons or pears
and inside the monument

are three cellars
and inside the cellars

are three skeletons
and inside

the skeletons inside
the cellars are three

more radiant
atomic absences.

MONUMENT XVII

She is colossal
as a drugged
cave,

a running boy
among us,
grown from accretion

of salt deposits,
more or less resistance
to lead.

I am embarrassed
by my self-
incivility,

garlic-skunking
deeper in the pine wood -
is it wildlife

or a row of pylons,
a weapon or
my revolting feelings,

my scummy politics
cracking open
her ribs like trees.

MONUMENT XVIII

I am your audience always
dismantled &
leaving a trace:

triangle cut-out
crotch like a cheese
re-enactment

on the chair,
in the cinema,
wax ruffle iterable.

Reeling in your
giant blue
speech-act.

I should push open
the skin egg,
I should crumble

the piano out
the window to
rapturous applause,

all the cows lain down
on the mountain
to think.

Call it a show,
call it a monument,
call it dissent.

MONUMENT XX

Who fell
asleep intact
amongst the
haunted anatomies:

crabs and claws,
orbs and sceptres,
dismembered
armatures.

Women, their
faces
bleached off
in the cemetery.

Trees torn up
and most
of the memory.
They say

desecration
is a form of
vigilance,
just bruised my skin

with my own
self-monument.
Off to meet
death

of the built-up
situation,
of the isolated
conversation.

Like crows on
a watermelon,
this particular plot
of churning motion.

THE SECRET COUNTRY OF HER MIND
LETTER TO JACQUI
EMILY BERRY

A response to Jacqui Kenny's photoseries The Agoraphobic Traveller, *a collection of otherworldly screenshots taken in remote locations in Google Street View.*

Over a number of years our lives had become increasingly constrained by a series of anxieties and phobias which we could not seem to get under control. What we feared primarily was the onset of an overpowering feeling we could not name. We called it 'panic', but – although any sight of this word invariably caused faint tendrils of the feeling to begin to unfurl inside us – the term was completely inadequate. It was not an active feeling, but something that opened in us when the conditions were right, like a night-blooming flower – and it could always, at any moment, be night.

*

Dear Jacqui,

My favourite thing about your pictures is the way their locations seem both familiar and strange, as if they're postcards from places I've visited in a dream. It is in the nature of postcards not to solicit a response; in their 'pure' form, let's say, they are dispatches from the road, where the sender has no permanent place; messages from the past. *This was the aim of the experiments: to send emissaries into Time, to summon the Past and Future to the aid of the Present... If they were able to conceive or dream another time, perhaps they would be able to live in it.* Your postcards received many replies, and this is mine.

*

The most crucial thing to avoid, or at the very least to carefully supervise, was being at any distance from home. Should this distance ever extend beyond the boundaries we had deemed manageable, we would be beset by an invincible vertigo, a vast and smothering homesickness. 'How I wish I could accept your invitation & pay you a visit to Sandown,' wrote Charles Darwin to his cousin William Fox in 1872, 'but I have long found it impossible to visit anywhere; the novelty & excitement would annihilate me.' Our terrified adhesion to a physical home was a faulty cure for an internal lostness, a failure to locate or keep close to an inner home, whose distance from us was incalculable; it might have been there somewhere, in the deep ocean of the soul, but it was unverifiable, just a rumour.

*

Intermittent spells of this sickness, 'this prolonged private state of emergency and curfew', to borrow writer Mina Nagy's description of his agoraphobia (which was the name given to this condition), ran

closer and closer together until the situation became chronic; attempts at treatment embarked upon with enthusiasm fell by the wayside and our belief in that chimera 'recovery' diminished to a dot of light like the last vestiges of signal fading from the screen of a vintage TV. The feeling felt as old and uncanny as that vintage TV, familiar even to those who have not known such an object as a brand new thing, because the past will not leave us alone. Stubbornly anachronistic in any setting, *out of harmony with the present*, heavy in the corner of the room.

> Anxiety is called the weightless, boundless width!
> – Kim Hyesoon, tr. Don Mee Choi, *Autobiography of Death*, 2018

*

The word *agoraphobia* is itself a kind of anachronism, coined in 1871 by the German psychiatrist Karl Friedrich Otto Westphal to describe symptoms he had encountered in several patients – acute anxiety in public spaces. Since its inception as a diagnosis, agoraphobia and its frequent companion panic disorder have undergone numerous iterations. 'On a certain level the concept of agoraphobia is a metaphor – a window into our culture and social relations,' writes Shelley Z. Reuter in her book on the subject, bringing to mind also the window that agoraphobics, when depicted, are often shown peering from anxiously. In our case, though there were numerous fearsome situations, what we feared most of all was travel. I use the term agoraphobia for want of any other way of describing it, but I am ambivalent about this business of naming. As the Norwegian author Tarjei Vesaas noted, 'One is not freed by mere words.'

*

As is customary in the naming of phobias, Westphal used a word from the Ancient Greek to denote the source of the fear, in this case *agora*.

In his book *On Kissing, Tickling and Being Bored* (1993), Adam Phillips remarks,

> The agora, after all, was the ancient place where words and goods and money were exchanged. Confronted with an open space... the agoraphobic fears that something nasty is going to be exchanged: one state of mind for another, one desire for another. But the phobia ensures a repression of opportunity, a foreclosing of the possibilities for exchange.

While I was writing this I went to see a new play at the Hampstead Theatre in London, sitting, of course, in a seat close to an aisle. *Unknown Rivers* by Chinonyerem Odimba tells the story of a young woman, Nene, struggling to overcome agoraphobia. 'It all flows too fast and everything washes away', is how Nene tries to explain her panic attacks to her best friend. To step into the flow of the agora is to accept the loss that is entailed in exchange, to bear the fact that things can and will flow away from us. Odimba's play invokes the water spirit Mami Wata, an African deity with multiple identities known for possessing both healing and destructive powers; she is like 'a river that never rests'. It is only through yielding to this continual movement – *going with the flow* – that Nene is able to return to the world. 'We carry the river, its body of water, in our body,' writes the poet Natalie Diaz.

> We must submerge, come under, beneath those once warm red waters now channeled blue and cool, the current's endless yards of emerald silk wrapping the body and moving it, swift enough to take life or give it.

Sigmund Freud suffered from agoraphobia. Psychoanalyst Theodor Reik, a former student, recalled an encounter with him in Vienna sometime after Freud's seventieth birthday:

> When we crossed a street that had heavy traffic, Freud hesitated as if he did not want to cross. I attributed the hesitancy to the caution of the old man, but to my astonishment he took my arm and said, "You see, there is a survival of my old agoraphobia, which troubled me much in younger years."

In these younger years, as described by Scott Stossel in *My Age of Anxiety* (2014), Freud would arrive for a train journey hours early, travelling in a separate compartment from his family 'because he was ashamed to have them witness his fits of anxiety'. While he attributed this 'neurosis' to a (conjectured) childhood experience of seeing his mother naked on a train, others have more convincingly linked it to his first experience of rail travel aged three, which was bound up with the loss of his first home and separation from his beloved nanny.

'Travellers, whether they acknowledge it or not, are travelling towards death,' Phillips writes elsewhere. Or, as the poet CAConrad puts it, 'There is no way to prevent the cost of living a day as the loss of that day, closer all the time to no more days.' But we thought we could prevent it by standing still.

*

I rode the waves flat out in a rowboat

bound for open sea ; sick & starved I kept

my eyes tight shut against the burning dark

against the lonely sun ; just prayed so long

I'd feel at last the thud of something firm

against my back & that it would be land

*

She exclaimed: Oh Madonna, an expression I had never heard her use. What's wrong, I asked. Gasping for breath, she cried out that the car's boundaries were dissolving, the boundaries of Marcello, too, at the wheel were dissolving, the thing and the person were gushing out of themselves, mixing liquid metal and flesh. She used that term: dissolving boundaries.

... She muttered that she mustn't ever be distracted: if she became distracted real things, which, with their violent, painful contortions, terrified her, would gain the upper hand over the unreal ones, which, with their physical and moral solidity, pacified her; she would be plunged into a sticky, jumbled reality and would never again be able to give sensations clear outlines. A tactile emotion would melt into a visual one, a visual one would melt into an olfactory one, ah, what is the real world, Lenù, nothing, nothing about which one can say conclusively: it's like that. And so if she didn't stay alert, if she didn't pay attention to the boundaries, the waters would break through, a flood would rise, carrying everything off...
– Elena Ferrante, tr. Ann Goldstein, *The Story of the Lost Child*, 2015

*

'Twenty-first-century culture is marked by... anachronism and inertia,' the cultural theorist Mark Fisher has argued. 'But this stasis has been buried, interred behind a superficial frenzy of "newness", of perpetual movement.' We find ourselves unable to keep moving, the way our century demands; we can't keep our own anachronism and inertia underground. When panic arrives it feels familiar but old, out of date (*not you again*), relentlessly current. It has disinterred itself – it stirs abroad while we stay stuck at home.

In her book *Enduring Time* (2017), an exploration of the relationship between time and care, Lisa Baraitser writes that modern time itself contains within it obdurate strands of the anachronistic; of slowed, still or stuck time... we appear to be holding our breath, *waiting*, not for a pending catastrophic "event", but for a diffuse catastrophe that has already happened to predictably play itself out.

In such a way could the movement of time be apprehended in panic, where time's emulsion becomes revoltingly unmixed, those 'strands of the anachronistic' clumping to the surface. *Harp not on that string, madam; that is past.* The Swiss author Fleur Jaeggy wrote that fear is 'something irrevocable'. A stone sunk deep in the mud suddenly rises. '[P]erfect stones', in the words of the poet Stanley Kunitz, 'rolled out of glacial time'.

*

For a long time I experienced the quality of the dark in my city as something untrustworthy. When I went out in the evening it felt as though I were emerging in the dead of night or doing something profoundly at odds with the preferences of my body and mind. The warmth emanating from lit interiors did not comfort me but only reinforced my sense of alienation. I used to believe that if you write things down you can keep them away from you. So far this has not proved to be true. As my mind turns again and again through the possible panaceas or poultices I might apply to my psychic wound – hitherto impervious to every style of mind and body therapy you could care to name – I must contemplate the final truth that pain is indestructible and it is with a kind of relief that I recognise this epiphany, one I have had many times before and which never fails to seem like news to me.

*

'Is it not possible –' asked Virginia Woolf, 'I often wonder – that things we have felt with great intensity have an existence independent of our minds – are in fact still in existence?'

Panic can seem to collect in the places it's been experienced, leaving as it were a viscous residue. Even years on, passing through such a place en route elsewhere, I sometimes feel its sticky pull. (*Platzschwindel*, 'place dizziness', was another German-speaking psychiatrist's name for agoraphobia.) Re-encountering these still-existing moments can feel like being shunted back in time, yet this sense of displacement is in most respects imperceptible, just the faintest change in atmospheric conditions.

If something hurts me, I erase it from my mental map. Places where I stumbled, fell, where I was struck down, cut to the quick, where things were painful – such places are simply not there any longer...

Whenever I have to visit one of these non-existent places (I try not to bear grudges), I've become like an eye that moves like a spectre in a ghost town.

– Olga Tokarczuk, tr. Jennifer Croft, *Flights*, 2018

Jacqui, your photos often seem to register this shift, the estranged camera angle keeping us aloof from the scene that nonetheless feels rather intimate. As Alberto Garcia-Magdaleno notes of your work,

> The point of view is always higher, resulting in a form of gigantism, in which all the human subjects become small figurines on a make-believe stage, even when up close.

And then there is the light: desert light, at once heavenly and disquieting, piercing and hazy, the invisible sun high in the monotone sky, intensity of brightness with its uncanny combination of alienation and welcome. You told me that most of your images were of places in group B of the Koppen climate classification, which are dry and semi-arid, defined by little precipitation. You feared the desert – *a desolate, barren region, waterless and treeless* – because of its emptiness, its farawayness, its dissolving boundaries. But you loved it too. I also feared and loved the desert. Some things do grow there.

> There's a certain Slant of light,
> Winter Afternoons —
> That oppresses, like the Heft
> Of Cathedral Tunes —
>
> Heavenly Hurt, it gives us —
> We can find no scar,
> But internal difference —
> Where the Meanings, are —

The poet Emily Dickinson is another master at transcribing these quiet shifts that leave 'no scar' yet effect untold changes within. In a letter to her mentor Thomas Higginson in 1862, she describes how poetry offers her a kind of release from this 'Heavenly Hurt' and the stuckness brought on by her sensitivities:

> And when, far afterward, a sudden light on orchards, or a new fashion in the wind troubled my attention, I felt a palsy here, the verses just relieve.

Sometimes we depress ourselves by thinking that there is no cure for our suffering. And we may give up for a time and stop looking. But we should never stop looking – I don't mean looking for the cure, I mean just looking, which is a way of travelling while standing still. Patrick Kavanagh said, 'To know fully even one field or one land is a lifetime's experience', a reminder that to study whatever is close at hand can also broaden our horizons. 'We know that writers, like readers,' writes Tara Bergin, 'perform their acts of transportation regardless of any physical distance they may travel: Emily Dickinson; Joseph Cornell (their open cages).'

There is a weird and beautiful cycle of poems about open cages by the Serbian poet Vasko Popa, called *The Little Box*. In Charles Simic's translation, the first poem opens:

> The little box gets her first teeth
> And her little length
> Little width little emptiness
> And all the rest she has.

Your pictures are like this little box, with their 'little width little emptiness', containing everything they need. *And all the rest she has*. 'I was depressed and sad for many days until I saw your pictures,' someone wrote to you. The imagination is a little box, a space of potentially infinite dimensions despite its apparent physical size within the mind of whoever it belongs to.

*

I told you I'd been playing the videogame *Gris*, a gorgeously animated platformer following a lightly drawn female figure through a series of landscapes which start out black and white and are gradually suffused with colour the further she advances along her journey. Accompanied by a melancholy soundtrack that quietly soared and dipped, I walked through deserts of fog and wind scattered with broken statues and the ruins of colonnades; I climbed the vertiginous staircases of baroque tumbledown palaces and fell from their bell towers; I leapt across canopies of disappearing trees and plunged into upside-down pools and flooded caverns. Wherever I went I was followed by shoals of light. I had very little experience of gaming and didn't know a game could feel like a metaphor for life or for the life of the mind, that it could even feel like a kind of self-help. It took me a long time to work out the puzzles that would release the girl out of one landscape and into a new one and many times when I was stuck I thought of giving up but I was compelled by the beauty of this virtual world to keep trying. Often when I found the way through it seemed as though the path or doorway had been right there all along and I just hadn't, somehow I hadn't *seen* it. The metaphor was obvious but still it charmed me. In a discussion thread on Steam about interpretations of *Gris*, one user posts,

> I'm confident everyone who's played the game has their own versions of what th' heck is going on, but as for "is it real"? I figure

the feelings are real. The *journey* is real.

> We travel far in thought, in imagination or in the realm of mem-
> ory. Events happened as they happened, not all of them of course
> but here and there a memory, or a fragment of a dream-picture is
> actual, is real, is like a work of art or is a work of art.
> – H.D., *Tribute to Freud*, 1970

*

Charles Simic also wrote a book of prose poems (another kind of little
box) inspired by the work of Joseph Cornell, a surrealist artist who
himself made little boxes, in his case shadow boxes displaying careful
arrangements of found objects. Cornell was not agoraphobic, as far as I
know, but he did not travel outside his city and spent almost his entire
life in New York. Yet Cornell was fascinated by travel, a feeling he
released into his boxes. In his diary he describes 'An abstract feeling
of geography and voyaging I have thought about before of getting
into objects'. 'Though he longed for larger horizons,' Olivia Laing has
observed,

> he didn't attempt to physically escape his circumstances, choosing,
> rather, to master the hard knack of conjuring infinite space from
> a circumscribed realm.

Probably we are all, in our own ways, attempting to master this hard
knack. So much can happen inside a little box. You can 'Make space voy-
ages inside her / Gather stars make time squirt its milk / And sleep in the
clouds'. *The journey is real.* The imagination, we know, is responsible for
bad dreams as well as good ones – our angels and our devils live side by
side. 'Oh god, I could be bounded in a nutshell, and count myself a king
of infinite space, were it not that I have bad dreams', Hamlet famously
said. Mary Ruefle reminds us of this in her essay *On Imagination* (2017):
if we praise imagination for its potential to set us free, we cannot forget
how it imprisons us too.

> And now, if I might depress you for a moment, I want to remind
> you that it is imagination that kicks in every morning when you
> wake and every night when you go to sleep and tells you that
> you are safe and all your loved ones are safe and all your belong-
> ings really do belong to you and are safe as you are safe.
>   Of course you are not safe, nor is anyone you know safe and
> nothing really belongs to you, not forever, your most beloved
> keepsake will one day belong to another. But who wants to live
> in insecurity and fear?

*

The poet Claudia Rankine has written of the very real and horrifying
power of 'the racial imaginary' in her collection of prose poems *Citizen:*

An American Lyric (2014), which documents the daily discrimination, threat and violence faced by people of colour. Opposite a page bearing the names of black Americans murdered in the USA by police, vigilantes and white supremacist terrorists, these now much-quoted lines appear: 'because white men can't / police their imagination / black men are dying'. In 2017 Rankine set up The Racial Imaginary Institute, an organisation devoted to the 'democratised exploration of race', whose masthead states: 'Our name "racial imaginary" is meant to capture the enduring truth of race: it is an invented concept that nevertheless operates with extraordinary force in our daily lives, limiting our movements and imaginations.'

> [T]he literature on agoraphobia, all published out of the developed West, historically has reflected – through its silence on race – a (normative) predominance of agoraphobia among married, educated, middle-class white women.
>
> In this context the findings of a relatively recent epidemiological study on agoraphobia are especially striking... that incidence of agoraphobia (and other phobias) were greater among African American women with the lowest socioeconomic status than among groups of white women.
> – Shelley Z. Reuter, *Narrating Social Order: Agoraphobia and the Politics of Classification*, 2007

*

'What kind of house does a man who has lived in a six foot by nine foot cell for over thirty years dream of?' In *Enduring Time* I read about the political prisoner Herman Wallace, a victim of the racial imaginary, who had been serving a prison sentence for armed robbery when he was indicted in the killing of a prison officer and subjected to an unfair trial. He was held in solitary confinement in Louisiana State Penitentiary for forty-two years before his conviction was finally overturned, only three days before his death in 2013. In 2001, Wallace received a letter from Jackie Sumell, an art student. This led to a lengthy collaboration, developed from the above question, which Sumell put to Wallace two years into the exchange. The details of this dream house were sketched out and elaborated on over fourteen years of letters, phone calls and meetings, from which Sumell created a 3D visualisation in AutoCAD with the aim of one day bringing the house to life. The destructive power of other people's 'bad dreams' had limited Wallace's movements to an extent that seems unendurable, but through this collaboration his imagination was released, opening up an infinite internal kingdom. '[This project] helps me to maintain what little sanity I have left, to maintain my humanity and dignity,' he said. 'It's probably the best move that I've ever made in my life.' Among the many features of his dream home, he specified, unsurprisingly, several defensive aspects, such as 'a trapdoor that leads down to an escape route' into a military-grade underground bunker; but he also includes a 'luscious rooftop garden... full of tomatoes, string beans, peas and other veggies as well as annual flowers such as gloxinia, delphinium, tulips and roses.'

Wallace's house, with its suggestion that for a prisoner even imagined

liberty is not free from constant vigilance against threat, recalls for me another imaginative dwelling, one which arose in vastly different circumstances. This is the garden known as Little Sparta, created by poet and 'avant-gardener' Ian Hamilton Finlay in partnership with Sue Finlay in the Pentland Hills, Scotland. Covering seven acres of moorland, Little Sparta combines structured landscaping and planting with a natural wildness and is populated by over 270 artworks created by Finlay and his collaborators, including sculpture in wood and stone, concrete poetry, pools and temples. Finlay was agoraphobic for much of his adulthood (interestingly he is said to have been freed from the condition following a stroke late in life), and Little Sparta became a kind of sanctuary for him. The poet Alice Oswald, who applied for a job as gardener at Little Sparta and recalls being interviewed by Finlay while she rowed the two of them back and forth across its small lake, has commented,

> It's an unsettling place, both protective and disruptive. One moment you move among birch trees where a set of pan pipes, half-hidden in leaves, tells you: "When the wind blows / venerate the sound"; the next moment you meet a stone tortoise on whose shell is written "panzer leader". There's a pool of reflected clouds, a broken column, a path of boat names; then suddenly gateposts topped with hand grenades leading to a huge decapitated head of Apollo. A submarine's conning tower sticks up out of the shallows of a very small lake... what are people meant to make of all this paradox?

Jacqui, your world too contains such paradoxes: the hopeful shots of animals grazing in unforgiving conditions, who on closer inspection are found to have their legs tied; the lonely glamour of abandoned dwellings which turn out to have devastating back stories; festivity amid desolation. And then there's the source – the all-seeing 'nine eyes' of the Google cars. 'Right now, I could name at least ten ideas I would have found intolerable or incomprehensible and frightening,' wrote poet and civil rights activist Audre Lorde, except as they came after dreams and poems. Poetry is not only dream and vision; it is the skeleton architecture of our lives. It lays the foundations for a future of change, a bridge across our fears of what has never been before.

Earlier in his life, overwhelmed by what he called his 'nervous trouble', Finlay had written to a friend, 'Sometimes I realise that I am at the world's mercy because of being ill, and that to be settled is only a dream.' This dream seems to have been realised through the creation of Little Sparta. Herman Wallace's house never had the opportunity to transcend the imaginative realm, yet it was much more than 'only a dream'. Discussing her collaboration with Wallace in a documentary film directed by Angad Singh Bhalla, *Herman's House* (2013), Jackie Sumell comments:

> I'm not a lawyer and I'm not rich and I'm not powerful but I'm an artist. I knew the only way I could get [Herman] out of prison was to get him to dream.

Take care of the little box, Vasko Popa warns us. *For God's sake / Don't let her get out of your sight.*

*

I felt I was born in a time when a lot of stuff
was just... not known... So we asked,
what was it like, to be a human being...?
The clouds flushed with their
ridiculous secret, light.
Our minds like a playing field in spring...
Most feelings are very old, they have
been under the earth and then up
to the surface again, they have been
in the vapour of clouds and all across
the surface of the sky like hairline cracks
in the glaze on porcelain, our motivations
under the river like pebbles or like the lives
of unseen creatures that keep us alive...
There was a song we had never heard before,
it was a very old song, it was a song
we once knew but an imaginary one.
Listening to it was like looking at the sky
at a certain time of day, on certain days,
in midsummer, as it slowly pulls itself apart.
There were so many times I wanted to give up
but then a message would appear
from a complete stranger, from miles away,
telling me to go on. So I went on.

*

'The contents of the unconscious need to be approached again and again,' Lisa Baraitser explains, 'chronically, often over many years, going over the same material in order to work away at psychic resistances, the chronic temporality of what Freud calls the "passive inertia" of psychic life.'

For a number of years, I saw a psychoanalyst twice a week. At the end of each session she would announce, 'It's time.' I began to view this not just as a notification that today's session had concluded, but as a definitive pronouncement on my condition: it's time, as in, time is to blame for all your problems; and/or, more positively perhaps, it is time that will lead to their resolution. It struck me that my fear of travel was, in a way, a fear of time. *Closer all the time to no more days.* How long will the journey take, how far (how many minutes or hours) away from home are we, how long will the panic go on for? A shorter journey always being infinitely preferable to a longer one. *This vertigo of space and reality*, says the narrator in Chris Marker's film *Sans Soleil* (1983), *stands for the vertigo of time*. We knew how long it took to get from one stop to the next on certain train lines, the shortest possible length of a given flight. There was the question of what was endurable. To *endure*, relating to *duration*, one's continued existence in time. So many times we thought the panic would destroy us, but we endured it, time and again. We were *made hard*, which is what the word originally meant, like the stone that rises, that lives longest in time.

> [A]fter all, time isn't "actual". When it seems long to you, then it is long; when it seems short, why, then it is short. But how long, or how short, it actually is, that nobody knows.
> – Thomas Mann, tr. H.T. Lowe-Porter, *The Magic Mountain*, 1927

*

Jacqui, you may have gathered that when I write to you I am also writing to myself. When we cannot approach something directly, we go at it another way. It can be helpful to believe that inertia is not always what it seems; that stuckness can be a cover for tectonic movement (Warning: deep excavation). We may think we're going nowhere, but we're hurtling through space. Scientists used to assume that there was little life in the ocean's deep layer, 1,000 fathoms down, where hardly any light penetrates. 'Even in the twentieth century scientists continued to imagine that life at great depth was insubstantial, or somehow inconsequential,' comments Tim Flannery in the *New York Review of Books* – but it is teeming down there. Among the otherworldly species discovered in the deeps is a creature that looks like 'a vermilion flame in a cage of ice'. We're looking for our own frozen flame. 'The ocean depths are not some hellish and distant zone,' Flannery adds, '[they are] connected in very intimate and immediate ways to ourselves.'

*

One day, ever more hampered by our unforgiving condition, you suddenly started travelling. Not in the usual way, of course, but virtually (by what measure are we casting 'usual', anyway? Less than twenty per cent of the world's population has ever set foot on a plane). *What a joy it is, so full of anticipation, to set out into the night. Where will it take me this time? Which country will I discover tonight?* You travelled the way one does in a videogame, but without rules or an objective, no inventory. You didn't know why you were doing it; you called it a 'deep impulse'. Your own response to the Heavenly Hurt. You were a time-traveller, a transhumanist, an alchemist, a modern-day explorer, any of the ways people described your activities after the fact. 'Perhaps some of us have to go through dark and devious ways before we can find the river of peace or the highroad to the soul's destination,' wrote Joseph Campbell, a mythologist who didn't believe a woman could be the hero of her own journey. Or there's Stanley Kunitz, writing on his own journey back in time: 'It is necessary to go through / dark and deeper dark, / and not to turn.'

*

If the subject of a picture taken with an eye behind the lens is loved by that eye, these pictures taken by the automated cameras of the Google cars must have been so lonely until your eye found them. You called them 'rescue images'. You would see them in the distance, giving off some kind of otherworldly light like a videogame collectible, or an undiscovered sea creature. 'The moment I had a feeling about the beauty of an image I would audibly "gasp",' you said, referencing what photographer Joel Meyerowitz calls 'the gasp reflex': 'That's where the picture is hidden in plain sight... Our gasp is inspiration... You charge the brain with a flush of oxygen, you immediately perceive yourself and the world in a new relationship.'

How many other virtual travellers had clicked down those abandoned roads and not even looked their way? It may be that a thing that has been lonely a long time never fully loses its loneliness. But, as Ocean Vuong has written, 'remember, / loneliness is still time spent / with the world', while Anne Michaels suggests, 'Perhaps loneliness is the real proof that we belong to something greater than ourselves, the way absence is proof of what once was a presence.' A woman wrote to tell you that, inspired by your work, she had visited her old house on Street View. Her cat, who had died some years ago, was there in the picture. 'She would be waiting for me to come home from school or work for ten years.'

*

"You don't like to travel," said Miss Goering, staring at her.

"It doesn't agree with me. I tried it that once. My stomach was upset and I had nervous headaches all the time. That was enough. I had my warning."

"I understand perfectly," said Miss Goering.

– Jane Bowles, *Two Serious Ladies*, 1943

You and I avoided travelling, but we still dreamt of travelling, and they were bad dreams. We would find ourselves on a plane that had taken off without our knowledge, and the journey ahead was long. We were on a train and had missed our stop, or in an underground carriage inside a tunnel that seemed too small for us to pass through. To be enclosed not once but twice. The walls of this tunnel were always lined with shadowy pipes and wires which seemed like something we shouldn't have been permitted to see, the inner workings of the city, strangely visceral and vulnerable to damage; a *hellish and distant zone.* Sometimes, not often, another train carriage would rear up out of nowhere and then disappear, its lighted windows briefly hovering in the darkness, like the ghost of an earlier journey. (*Surely the most distinctive feature of life in the depths is the frequency with which it creates its own light.*) This made us feel less alone. *In some way you make me feel accompanied,* someone wrote to you in another message. Perhaps this was what Joseph Campbell called 'the appearance of the willing helper at the critical moment' in your personal myth; or were you the willing helper in someone else's myth?

*

In one of your pictures there is a woman in a red coat standing at the edge of a wooded path. She appears small, and something in her aspect makes me see her first as a child. Perhaps it's the perspective, the way we look down at her from a height. She's looking back towards the camera, as if to lead the way. Her face is blurred, like all the faces in these photos. 'Do faceless images emit sound?' Tina Campt asks in her book *Listening to Images* (2017). 'If so, at what frequencies do they register? If not, what can we apprehend in and through their muteness?' We do not know her, will most likely never know her. But we are all 'citizens of photography', in the words of Ariella Azoulay, who argues in *The Civil Contract of Photography* (2008), particularly in reference to the documentation of suffering, for the responsibility of spectators towards the photographed. The subject of a photograph, she maintains, imagines a future in which someone sees their suffering and takes action. What if there is suffering in an image which cannot be seen (or is mute), the way we cannot tell which of the houses in your images have happy stories or sad ones? I see this woman looking our way, as if caught in the moment of imagining us in the future. Our action is to imagine her in return. Susan Sontag said that 'To take a photograph is to participate in another person's (or thing's) mortality, vulnerability, mutability', but I do not know where these things go when we make the person into a symbol. It is hard to live in the real world. Sontag also said that a photo was a memento mori, but someone pointed out on Reddit that people get to live forever on Google Maps. 'What the Photograph reproduces to infinity has occurred only once,' commented Roland Barthes: 'the Photograph mechanically repeats what could never be repeated existentially.' Again and again she waits for us at the edge of the path. I am listening, to see if we can hear her. 'The source of poetry', Anne Michaels writes, 'is intensely private, but it is not personal – poetry must lead the reader not to the poet's life, but to the reader's own.' I do not know what the source of photography is, or to whose life the woman in the red coat leads us. All our lives are unknowable, but still we try to know them. What happens to a body when it becomes a sign? It's autumn and the trees are anointed with yellow, the leaves are thick on the ground. She is waiting for us to catch up with her and we will, one day.

*

You trod your lonely path and I trod mine,
and no one would drink from my tap but me,
this water which wouldn't stop flowing.
Irrevocably, the born arrive, and they can't
be put back, no, but who on earth would want
to put them back. I reached a door, passed
through it, reached another door, and so it
went on, there was nobody at home to greet me.
Once I saw someone I thought I knew.
What if just under this layer of life you could
find the old one, moving forward just the same,
and just above, what's yet to come, would I
know myself if I met me now, coming the other
way back then. I couldn't think of any reason.
When she had something painful to tell, it was usually
her way to introduce it among a number of disjointed
particulars, as if it were a medicine that would
get a milder flavour by mixing. I've been watching
a tall thin tree bending over and back
in the wind. Mama mia, how can anyone bend
so much without breaking? I said I had been lost
in a fantasy world in which I could travel freely.
She said the fantasy world was this one.
At the hour of my death I did not die,
but was born again in this life.

*

The picture of the house in the marshes summons my eye again and again. A house like a child's drawing, white with two windows and a gabled roof, sailing in a sea of reeds that billow forwards, their tousled heads touched by light. They could be a crowd carrying their idol. The house tilts back, its front elevation lit by an unseen sun. A seal-coloured sky bleeds to a dark horizon of distant trees and dwellings. To the left a wedge of silver shines through the grasses like a sign.

> *You may ask yourself, "What is that beautiful house?"*
> *You may ask yourself, "Where does that highway go to?"*
> *You may ask yourself, "Am I right? Am I wrong?"*
> *And you may say to yourself, "My god! What have I done?"*

Whenever I looked at this image, even after I knew its story, I found it beautiful and somehow comforting. I did not register that the tilt of the house was, in fact, catastrophic, or that a house submerged in wetlands could no longer be a home. What do we fear most, if not loss? And yet, in art, loss is the source of so much beauty. *I cannot walk // on the moonlit leaves of ocean / down that white road alone.* How lucky we are to have something to lose. 'We were going to live here the rest of our lives,' said a former resident of the neighbourhood to which this house used to belong – a neighbourhood where thirteen homes were devastated by hurricane. 'We had no intention of ever leaving.' It is said that grief is the price we pay for love; we know, sooner or later, that we will lose everything (*nothing really belongs to you, not forever*). 'Let's face it. We're undone by each other. And if we're not, we're missing something,' writes Judith Butler in *Precarious Life: The Power of Mourning and Violence* (2004):

> This seems so clearly the case with grief, but it can be so only because it was already the case with desire. One does not always stay intact.

Until then, however much we might try to let go, we hold on.

> . . . . Murderers are easy
> to understand. But this: that one can contain
> death, the whole of death, even before
> life has begun, can hold it to one's heart
> gently, and not refuse to go on living,
> is inexpressible.
> – Rainer Maria Rilke, tr. Stephen Mitchell, 'The Fourth
> Elegy', 1923

Gently I hold it to my heart, with all that has been lost, and all that is yet to be, the white house born aloft by its grasses.

*

I had grown so tired of the formula 'Face your fears'. As if fear were a mirror you could look directly into, or as if fear *weren't* a mirror you could look into, complete with a mirror's tricks, which pretends to show you the world just as it is but gets everything backwards.

One is not saved by mere words. Or is it that the words are not the right ones? Some words I prefer are quoted by the Buddhist teacher Pema Chödrön in her book *When Things Fall Apart* (1996): 'I once asked the Zen master Kobun Chino Roshi how he related with fear, and he said, "I agree. I agree."'

What is a phobia for? In his foreword to Maryanne M. Garbowsky's *The House without the Door: A Study of Emily Dickinson and the Illness of Agoraphobia* (1989), John Cody remarks, 'It seems undeniable, for instance, that [Dickinson's] anxieties had a protective effect and safe-guarded not only the poetry, but her person as well.'

On a rare trip abroad I bought a postcard, a sketch of a downcast-looking child wearing a hoodie with a slogan on it: *Take pride in your fears.* I did not know what it might mean or look like to take pride in one's fears, but I thought it must be better than being ashamed of them. You and I have spent so many years wrestling with (and concealing) our affliction, the grand arch-enemy who looms over our lives; we never stopped to wonder if we might in fact be getting something out of this exchange.

'I had always hoped that I might develop a bona fide phobia', writes Sophie Collins in her book *Small White Monkeys: On Self-expression, Self-help and Shame* (2018) – a sentence I read with some surprise. Was it possible that this condition which we so yearned to disown or eject could be something to wish for? Recalling a youthful interest in shows about phobic people overcoming their fears, Collins describes how, contrary to the show's intentions, she would experience 'pure disap-pointment' at the moments when the protagonists were released from their phobias:

> The owner of the phobia had surrendered something that I deemed covetable. Which was what, exactly? A phobia not only made someone unusual, but someone who had to be catered for, looked after and considered, through no ostensible fault of her own.

In Greek mythology Phobos – from whose name, meaning 'fear', the word *phobia* derives – was the son of Aphrodite and Ares, goddess of love and god of war. Phobos is a minor god and does not appear as a character in any myths, but his face – and that of his twin brother Deimos (Dread) (quite a family!) – is depicted in the shields of those who worshipped him, such as that of Herakles, described here by the Greek poet Hesiod (in H.G. Evelyn-White's translation):

> In his hands [Herakles] took his shield, all glittering: no one ever broke it with a blow or crushed it. And a wonder it was to see; for its whole orb was a-shimmer with enamel and white ivory and electrum, and it glowed with shining gold; and there were zones of cyanus drawn upon it. In the centre was Phobos worked in adamant, unspeakable, staring backwards with eyes that glowed with fire.

Some translations offer 'staring back' instead of 'staring backwards'. Whose fear is Phobos? If he is staring backwards he could be looking right back through the shield to Herakles himself; if he's staring back then it is Herakles' opponents who are struck mute by his flaming glance. Herakles' shield looks to me like a way of taking pride in one's fears, the 'whole orb a-shimmer' with gold and blue (*cyanus* is a glass paste of a deep blue colour), with fear in the centre, ready both to protect and terrify. Adamant, a stone of 'surpassing hardness', that which endures. You told me, 'I'm always drawn to images that have both a darkness and a lightness to them (lightness feels like hope to me) but the darkness is always there, it never goes away.' May we be as strong as Herakles' shield, as our fear, that we may meet its gaze in the mirror, our own gaze staring backwards.

*

Prophecy

<pre>
There were days   my sun would set
without ever   having been seen
the sky hung grey   & extraordinary
over smooth green lawns   I was so sad
& I did not think   my sadness
would ever stop   but one day
it did   I have seen the wind
agitate the trees   beyond all reason
you would not think   they could
stand it   but they stood it
whatever they could let go   they let go
</pre>

*

You emailed me to say you had been reading a book about homing pigeons. You joked that a homing pigeon could be our spirit animal, because of their attachment to home. In *Homing: On Pigeons, Dwellings, and Why We Return* (2019), Jon Day references biologist Rupert Sheldrake, who speculates that pigeons are 'connected to their lofts and the other members of their colony by a "kind of psychic elastic band" which allows them to travel to the ends of the earth while always allowing them to feel the pull of home.' We knew all about the pull of home, but in our case the pull was too strong. It had no interest in letting us travel to the ends of the earth; at certain distances we felt stretched almost to breaking point. *Why is it I can no longer bear travelling? Why is it I keep trying, like a lost child, to get home?*

When you were younger you experienced a strange phenomenon – a sense, when setting off for school, that you were tethered to home by elastic around your ankles. It would stretch and stretch until it was so tight you would have to physically lift your feet from the ground to be freed from it. In one of your pictures, a girl in a red jacket and blue jeans is walking away from us, down a track between rickety wooden fences and indeterminate dwellings. We do not know if she is leaving or coming back. The track is much-trodden, with a thin layer of snow at the edges. Almost directly above the girl, in a slanted rectangle of sky marked out by electricity lines, a bird is in flight, its path crossing hers. *Two drifters, off to see the world, there's such a lot of world to see... Wherever you're going, I'm going your way.* It is my favourite image.

Unless otherwise stated, poems included in the text are by Emily Berry. The untitled poems are excerpts from a long poem in progress called 'Unexhausted Time'. The sources of unattributed quotations are given here:

'The secret country of her mind' is taken from Sylvia Townsend Warner, *Lolly Willowes* (1926; Virago Modern Classics, 2012); *This was the aim of the experiments...* is taken from the script of *La Jetée* (dir. Chris Marker, 1962); Mina Nagy, 'A Portrait of the Artist as an Agoraphobe', sultansseal. com, 2018; Shelley Z. Reuter, *Narrating Social Order: Agoraphobia and the Politics of Classification* (University of Toronto Press, 2007); Tarjei Vesaas, tr. Elizabeth Rokkan, *The Ice Palace* (1963; Penguin Modern Classics, 2018); Natalie Diaz, 'The First Water Is the Body', in *Postcolonial Love Poem* (Faber, 2020); the Theodor Reik quotation is cited in Paul Carter, *Repressed Spaces: The Poetics of Agoraphobia* (Reaktion Books, 2002); Adam Phillips, 'On Risk and Solitude', in *On Kissing, Tickling and Being Bored* (Faber, 1994); CAConrad, 'Unknown Duration of Fear', in *Ecodeviance: (Soma)tics for the Future Wilderness* (Wave Books, 2014); Mark Fisher, *Ghosts of My Life: Writings on Depression, Hauntology and Lost Futures* (Zero Books, 2014); *Harp not on that string...* is from William Shakespeare, *Richard III*, IV.iv; Fleur Jaeggy, tr. Tim Parks, *Sweet Days of Discipline* (1991; And Other Stories, 2018); Stanley Kunitz, 'The Testing-Tree', in *The Testing-Tree* (Little, Brown, 1971); Virginia Woolf, 'Sketch of the Past', in *Moments of Being: Autobiographical Writings* (Pimlico, 2002); Alberto Garcia-Magdaleno, 'Feature: Photographer Jacqui Kenny', modernminimalmonochrome.com (27 July 2018); Emily Dickinson, 'There's a certain Slant of light', in *The Complete Poems* (Faber, 1976); Patrick Kavanagh cited in Jon Day, *Homing: On Pigeons, Dwellings, and Why We Return* (John Murray, 2019); Tara Bergin, 'Is Travel Writing Dead?', in *Granta: Journeys*, 138 (Winter 2017); Vasko Popa, tr. Charles Simic, *Vasko Popa* (NYRB Poets, 2019); the Steam user is @Jackalope_908, see steamcommunity.com/app/683320/discussions/(27 March 2019); Charles Simic, *Dime-store Alchemy: The Art of Joseph Cornell* (1992; NYRB Classics, 2011); Mary Ann Caws, ed., *Joseph Cornell's Theater of the Mind: Selected Diaries, Letters and Files* (Thames and Hudson, 1993); Olivia Laing, 'Joseph Cornell: How the reclusive artist conquered the art world — from his mum's basement', *Guardian* (25 July 2015); Alice Oswald quoted in Sarah Karmali, 'Inside Ian Hamilton Finlay's Enchanting Garden Little Sparta', *Harper's Bazaar* (12 May 2015); Audre Lorde, 'Poetry is not a luxury', in *Sister Outsider* (1984; Penguin Modern Classics, 2019); Ian Hamilton Finlay letter quoted in *Ian Hamilton Finlay: Selections* (1977; University of California Press, 2012); *I felt I was born in a time...* paraphrases Sharon Olds speaking on the Commonplace podcast, hosted by Rachel Zucker (episode 38, 4 October 2017); *There were so many times...* paraphrases Jacqui Kenny, private correspondence; *What a joy it is...* is a retranslation of Hélène Cixous, from *Dream I Tell You* (2003; Columbia University Press, 2006); Joseph Campbell, *The Hero with a Thousand Faces* (1949; New World Library, 3rd edition, 2012); 'Photography legend Joel Meyerowitz on how to take a good photo', *Front Row* (18 May 2018); Ocean Vuong, 'Someday I'll Love Ocean Vuong', in *Night Sky with Exit Wounds* (Copper Canyon Press, 2016); Anne Michaels, *Infinite Gradation* (House Sparrow Press, 2017); *Surely the most distinctive feature...* is from Tim Flannery, 'Where Wonders Await Us', *New York Review of Books* (20 December 2007); Susan Sontag, *On Photography* (Penguin, 1977); Roland Barthes, tr.

Richard Howard, *Camera Lucida: Reflections on Photography* (1980; Vintage, 1993); Anne Michaels, ibid.; *You may ask yourself...* is from the 1981 song 'Once in a Lifetime' by Talking Heads; *I cannot walk...* is from 'Sea Canes' by Derek Walcott, in *Selected Poetry* (Heinemann, 1993); 'We were going to live here...' is from the *New York Times* video 'Coming Back After Sandy: Kissam Avenue, Staten Island' (6 December 2012); *Why is it I keep trying...* is Roland Barthes, tr. Richard Howard, *Mourning Diary* (Hill and Wang, 2009); *Two drifters...* is from the 1961 song 'Moon River', composed by Henry Mancini with lyrics by Johnny Mercer.

INTERVIEW   INGRID POLLARD

Ingrid Pollard and I have joked that in one of her past lives she was an English country gentleman. I like to imagine her as one of the men Thomas Gainsborough might have painted: a confident young squire clad in a frock coat and accompanied at all times by an obedient hound. 'What do you think of those boots?' she once asked me during a train journey we took together. I looked out of the window in the direction she was pointing to see a figure on the platform wearing a Barbour jacket, jodhpurs and box calf riding boots. 'It's a look that would suit you very well,' I replied.

Ingrid's art is the foil for such a figure. Or rather, the enduring archetype of the English country gentleman, with his hereditary sense of belonging to the idealised rural landscape, is the foil for much of Ingrid's art. Her work began to attract attention in the late 1980s after *Pastoral Interlude* (1988), a series of five hand-tinted silver prints captioned with fragments of text. Aiming to disrupt the conception of the English countryside as the idyllic antidote to urban life and its chaotic social relations, *Pastoral Interlude* places a series of single figures, all of whom are black, against various rural backgrounds. The text highlights the sense of alienation, of un-belonging, that comes with being the only 'black face in a sea of white'. In the second to last image, a woman gazes out across the fields. Standing in profile with a serene facial expression, it is clear that she derives some pleasure from the verdant scenery that stretches in front of her. Yet she is blocked from total enjoyment of the place, both literally – a drystone wall sits between her and the landscape – and figuratively, in that racist ideologies of nationalism and heritage dictate that she will never be at home here.

Pastoral Interlude was followed by *The Cost of the English Landscape* (1989), a configuration of photographs, postcards, maps and collaged strips of text punctuated by wooden frames. The most recent installation of the work, at *The Lie of the Land*, an exhibition held at MK Gallery, Milton Keynes, in 2019, was flanked by signs that read 'KEEP OUT' and 'PRIVATE PROPERTY', sandwiched between a tripartite image of the artist traversing a stile to claim her place within that landscape. Although Ingrid's oeuvre includes found objects, video, wallpaper and textiles, she has always championed photography as a sensual and pictorial art form that, especially when confronting the workings of racism, can achieve so much more than mere documentation.

Talking to Ingrid, it is clear that she is drawn to what terrifies her. Words like 'frightening' and 'scary' come up often, reminding me of the 'unease' and 'dread' mentioned in the caption to the first image in *Pastoral Interlude*. Such feelings seem to energise Ingrid rather than deter her. She takes the fear that comes from walking in the Lake District alone, or encountering racist caricatures of black boys on pub signs, and transmutes it into a rare kind of beauty, a beauty that can accommodate the abrasive aspects of life while retaining its grace. The series *Self Evident* (1995) and *Near and Far* (2002) have a lightness to them that alleviates the bleaker poetry of her early works, showing her versatility as a portraitist and storyteller.

Ingrid was born in Georgetown, Guyana, in 1953 and migrated to London when she was four. She was my neighbour growing up on the street where I was born, and my earliest memories of her are as an inspiring person who was frequently away on walking or rowing trips. Getting to know her art as an adult gave me an even greater admiration for her adventurous spirit. In July I returned to this neighbourhood in Stroud Green, north London, to chat with her about her work in the context of the current political climate.   CORA GILROY-WARE

THE WHITE REVIEW The past few months have been an extraordinary chapter in the history of the fight against racism. Given the fact that we carry out so much of our lives online now, what are some of the most striking differences you see between anti-racist activism thirty years ago and anti-racist activism today?

INGRID POLLARD The thing that strikes me the most is the speed at which things change. An argument will rise up, or a response to something, like the statue of Edward Colston in Bristol, and then it dies down as quickly as it came and it's on to the next thing.

The internet is great for communication and getting stuff out. Without that video of George Floyd things would have been very different. With Rodney King, in 1991, we had a blurry clip of him being beaten up that resonated in a different kind of way, as an image of the horror of police brutality in a broader sense. The video of George Floyd's death showed a callous man committing murder. He was part of the police, but there was something else beyond police brutality. To have such a clear image of what was going on – at one point the man looks into the camera – that was a frightening moment. The clarity with which we can see these acts of violence is one of the biggest differences between then and now. Also the speed at which these crimes become known; we don't have to wait months or even years to hear about them. You hear about them immediately.

Personally, as an older woman, I find internet-led activism completely overwhelming. But I've been following it closely and contributing financially rather than going out into the street, like I did in the past. Going into the street doesn't feel appropriate now, for me. I've also been connecting with friends in the US where it seems completely out of control. To me it's important to be kind. So I have my own way of doing activism on the down-low.

TWR Has this last eruption of anti-racist efforts had an effect on your work?

IP Indirectly, yes it has. It's given a different flavour to what I'm doing. I'm currently working on a piece called *Palms*. When I began, I was thinking about a particular location in Devon, the jet stream and what grows there. Now I'm thinking more about things that get transported and how they come back. There's a lot of lace-making in this part of the South West because of the Protestants who came from Belgium and France during the sixteenth century. I heard a story of a white guy who was convicted of a crime, but his sister, who was well-to-do, made sure he wasn't put to death, but was sent to the Caribbean instead. Because she was involved with lace-making, she gave him a lot of lace to take to the plantation owners there, and he built up a thriving business selling it. And then lace became fashionable in plantations. Like lots of other commodities, lace moved around, became popular, and was transformed in the process. Most lace was made from cotton, which of course was grown, among other places, in the US. Sometimes lace was made from jute which, along with cotton, was also grown in India.

I've been thinking about lace doilies as a staple of Caribbean homes. Lace-makers sometimes look down on doilies as being low-class. But in black culture they were seen as beautiful. In some Nigerian weddings men wear lace which is really expensive. So I'm working with lace-makers. The piece is provisionally called *Palms*, because palm fronds and ferns were featured in very expensive lace until machinery came along and everybody lost their jobs. Doilies were mostly made by machines.

I recently visited the Museum of English Rural Life in Reading, and I was looking at the smocks that peasants wore. They were designed in a similar way to the smocks worn by enslaved people in the Caribbean, both men and women, in the mid-to-late nineteenth century. The fact that English peasants and Caribbean enslaved people wore the same design made perfect sense to me. Landowners would have brought that design to the colonies. I'm interested in these movements and the transformations they bring about. What's going on now with the fight against racism has underscored the politics of what I'm doing, which is great.

TWR I'm also fascinated by lace as a frothy, feminised fabric that seems anachronistic even though it's still in use. What you're saying makes me think that it has much in common with sugar, or rather confectionary, in the sense that it has delicate and refined associations, but behind its sensual properties is a history of violence that is obscured by its pleasures.

IP Sugar and lace are similar. Sugar has no nutritional value, and lace doesn't do anything. It doesn't keep you warm. It was used purely to show off how rich you were. There are versions of lace in lots of cultures.

TWR Let's return to the question of images. Has the shifting consumption of images, for example from print to screen, affected your practice? It must be strange to have witnessed photography becoming something to which everyone has access.
IP I get invited to do Instagram takeovers, which are very fleeting, but I feel people still want objects in exhibitions. When I started out taking pictures, it was a craft. Besides the move from film to digital, taking photographs as an artist requires a different sensibility to instant or one-off photography. But when I began, I wasn't expecting to have a career as an artist. I had a regular job. I worked for the council, as a gardener, cleaner, zoo worker, librarian, then in the evenings I did photography and drawing. That seemed a perfectly normal way to be. Photography was a hobby, but I managed to catch a wave of other people doing the same sort of thing. I didn't go to art school until I was about thirty, because I was working shit jobs. I had no career advice at school, and no guidance on applying to art college.

TWR A year or two ago I was at a talk given by Linton Kwesi Johnson in which he distinguished the Windrush Generation from what he called the 'Rebel Generation', the wave of Caribbean migrants who came to the UK slightly later as children or young adults, or who were the children of those who came during the Windrush era. While the Windrush Generation largely sought to assimilate into British culture, the Rebel Generation wanted to be seen and heard on their own terms. Do you consider yourself part of this 'Rebel Generation'? Did you feel like you were part of something rebellious when you got involved with photography?
IP Yes, sort of. The rebelliousness for me wasn't just about being from a migrant background, it was about being a woman, being queer and being working-class. From 1981 to around '85 I was a screen printer and photographer in a women's print collective that combined feminism, queer politics and black politics, all mixed together. It was linked to feminist publications like *Spare Rib* and *Outright*, so I made connections to lots of different people and groups. The first National Black Arts Convention was in 1982 at Wolverhampton Polytechnic; I took a holiday to Derby so I would be near it. For me back then, it was more about coming together than the idea of actually making change. It was more about gathering than being seen outwardly in a particular way. It was

inward-looking, if anything. When they had the first Black Women's Conference in 1979 and then the first Black Lesbian Conference shortly after I was like, 'Oh my god, we're all here!' It was about being together, not feeling like you only knew one or two black women who were politicised. So you met rebellious people, but they were also regular people doing regular jobs. We didn't consider ourselves rebels, but we weren't getting opportunities from the mainstream, so we did our own thing. It had never been done before, so it was new, and thrilling.

TWR What were the spaces that allowed you to come together?
IP I remember that the Black Women's Conference was at a youth centre in Tottenham. It was those kinds of places: community centres, schools. Eventually there were various women's centres in different locations where we could meet in groups. We did youth work, and 'girls work', which came out of youth work. Girls work was a feminist project that fostered self-esteem in young girls by allowing them to work with other (black) women who served as role models. There was an emphasis on learning skilled work, particularly technical work, which was associated with male power and knowledge. It also provided a safe space away from sexism, misogyny and unwanted interest. That's all disappeared now.

TWR For someone of my generation, it's hard not to hear what you're saying and feel like that was a lost golden age. I never had anything like that sense of a community. It sounds incredible to be alive at a time when people were coming together in physical space on that scale.
IP It wasn't as organised as it sounds; it was random and ad hoc. There was a whole alternative scene going on generally. I was squatting for a long time, from 1975 when I left my parents' house to about 1982. So the political and arts stuff was part of a broader counterculture, or however you want to call it.

TWR Do you have photos from when you were squatting?
IP Oh yeah! It was a very druggy scene. I wasn't into drugs but they were always around. The buildings were crumbling and there was detritus everywhere, and I think many of the people felt like they were seen as detritus as well. But overall

it was a nice atmosphere. Some people had stable jobs, but not many. I remember there was a woman who was really interested in looking after animals, one of the first to be invested in the liberation of animals. Another woman turned up with her horse. She put the horse in people's gardens and it made its way down the road through all the different gardens, eating grass and plants. It didn't seem bizarre at the time. It was a Welsh pony. This was in a squat in Penge. It was nice. I was working at Crystal Palace Zoo around that time as well, looking after animals and taking the mobile zoo and ponies out to events.

TWR Going back to the question of migration, it's important to consider these issues in the context of today, when people of Caribbean descent who have lived their whole lives in the UK are being faced with deportation to countries they haven't been to since childhood, or even at all. Has the Windrush scandal and general 'hostile environment' affected you?
IP My nieces immediately said, 'Where are your papers?' I said, 'Don't worry, I've got it covered, I know where the papers are, thankfully.' It's a terrible tactic, and it's all mixed in with what's happening to migrants moving across Europe. One minute Notting Hill Carnival is being celebrated, the next minute the contributions of migrants are made completely unimportant. None of it is surprising to me, though; there has always been some form of that exploitative sentiment in this country during my lifetime.

TWR As the grandchild of a Windrush migrant, I've often wondered what my generation would be called. Maybe we are the 'lost' generation, in the sense that many of us have never been to the Caribbean, and so are forced to find that sense of connection in our places of birth, which is made impossible by the racism of the government and the dominant culture more broadly. There is a lost piece. I've never been to Guyana, but I feel spiritually connected to the land where my grandmother came from. Have you been back to Guyana as an adult?
IP Yeah, a couple of times. I went back with my mother the first time, which was a bit weird. Ideally she would have gone back with my dad and they could have reminisced about the things they left behind, but he had died by then. I'd come to England when I was four, so didn't remember

anything. She got really annoyed after a while that I was basically just a tourist. Guyana is actually a big tourist spot now. It's very scary. They're bringing golf courses to the interior of the country, into that precious bit of rainforest. I've never been to the interior, I've just stayed in Georgetown, but I'd love to go. What stopped you from going?

TWR My father and grandmother were invested in carving out a Black British identity that was all about belonging in this country. In a way, Guyana is nothing to do with my life and who I am. But I can't help but feel like a part of me is missing. I'm not sure I would find the answers if I went to Berbice, though, which is the rural region where my family lived.
    At the multidisciplinary event we co-curated at MK Gallery in 2019 for the exhibition *The Lie of the Land*, we spoke about the various ways in which the rural landscape is objectified. Tourism is a theme in your work, isn't it?
IP Yes, tourism is a theme. *Seaside Series* (1989), for example, was taken in Hastings. I was interested in that particular location as a site of invasion by, and repelling of, William the Conqueror from Normandy, but it's also so close to London that you got a lot of black people going there for day trips. I'm interested in postcards, too, as part of the tourist's view of a place. They're throwaway, ephemeral, but carry essentialist ideas of the place. When I was growing up, you didn't see black people in the postcards that you bought on the high street, so I thought, I'll just make my own.

TWR So much of the conversation around racism now is focused on what so-called white people do to people of colour, and the idea that white people need to atone for their sins. I've been thinking a lot recently about the fact that this is a very superficial view that paradoxically elevates 'white people' and places that particular idea at the centre of the conversation. Racism is much, much more than that. I think one of the things that makes activism and genuine collaboration among people of different backgrounds so difficult at the moment is the way in which racism can exist within the body itself; it is deeply internalised and passed down, passed down through how people treat others, their children, how they treat themselves. To me, much of your work has traces of this internalised trauma. Is this something you've consciously engaged with?
IP That's a hard question. Something that I've

noticed is that the younger generation of black artists tend to come from West African rather than Caribbean backgrounds. On the whole, their work is celebratory, and they appear to have much more optimistic expectations for what they will achieve in the future. In terms of photography there is a lot more portraiture. It's about showing your power, and celebrating yourself in a very big way.

In the 1980s and 90s, a lot of the work by Caribbean-descended artists was imbued with a longing for a sense of home, an African ancestral home, and a sense of deep, deep sadness that that connection had been lost. And that was one of the central traumas, that we were snatched, or rather our ancestors were snatched and taken to another place. That deep longing is not always so visible in work by younger black artists. In fact, I think it's become quite alien. So it's strange to see art with this celebratory agenda being shown in England, a country built on a colonial attitude that produced the sense of longing found in the art of the older, 'rebel' generation. But the country itself has changed a lot.

TWR I want to ask you about race and photography. I've recently done some work on [US abolitionist, statesman and writer] Frederick Douglass and learned that in the nineteenth century, photography was heralded as an emancipatory technology that could help the struggle against racism by complicating the stereotypical images of blackness that had circulated in more traditional media. Photography showed the differences between black people, their individuality and therefore their humanity. Over time, however, photography became complicit in producing new racist stereotypes, so had the opposite effect. Mark Sealy speaks of this in his book *Decolonising the Camera: Photography in Racial Time* (2019). In works such as *Seaside Series*, was photography a way for you to address the stereotypical images of blackness that you saw in popular visual culture?
IP I've always thought of early photography as something that would have fostered stereotypes by transmitting impressions of people from Africa and the colonies back to the armchairs of Europe and the US. I've seen it as something that would have solidified these stereotypes, but perhaps I'm not thinking back far enough. I know that in Ethiopia photographic equipment had been brought there by Europeans in the late nineteenth century. The royal family then used photography

to craft a certain image of themselves as paternal rulers, which I thought was interesting.

With my own work, I'm very careful about the figurative images I put out into the world. It's a negotiation between me and the person I'm photographing. I focus on our relationship as sitter and photographer and not on how anyone else will interpret the image. Even though I've got the camera and the means of reproducing the image, I allow the person in front of the camera to have agency.

But stereotypes are important in my work. They've always felt like things I could use and explore. People are much more literate in stereotypes than they realise. If you subvert them even a little bit you can do something interesting. In the *Seaside Series*, there's a self-portrait that I took in front of a sweet machine with 'The Chocolate Machine' written on it. I always thought of that photo as uncomfortably funny in the way that it connects to the racist names I was called when I was little, 'chocolate bunny' and all that. It's about putting those associations front and centre, forcing a confrontation with them. It's provocative. Some people don't get it, of course. So those kinds of stereotypical images and associations are very useful because we unconsciously know how to read them. People are familiar with them, even if they like to think that they're not.

Stereotypes are just a shorthand. But when you think about them you realise how complicated that shorthand is, how it's been pushed for decades, in a sense becoming more refined over time. I like to work with stereotypes because, unfortunately, they are easily legible to white people, and to black people as well.

TWR I know that you have an archive of photos of black figures on pub signage from around the UK, some of which are in your book *Hidden in a Public Place* (2008).
IP I've been collecting those for about twenty-eight years. Did you see the 'gallows' sign that arches across the road in Nottingham, the Green Man & Black's Head? On top of the sign in the centre is a disembodied black head wearing a Moorish turban, double-sided, one side smiling, one side frowning. There have been many campaigns to get it removed, including a petition in the wake of the George Floyd killing. I think they've taken the head down and have hidden it somewhere.

The first sign I saw had a black figure that was

dressed in satin, bejewelled and decorated with pearls, and it was called The Black Boy. The bar also had a cocktail list with drinks called 'jungle bunny' this and that. This was a long time ago, in the late Seventies, early Eighties, near the Gower Peninsula in Wales. It frightened me how the racism was so out in the open, and it was also a selling ploy. It made clear who they expected their clientele to be: I felt they didn't want black people in there. I've gone back there since and they've changed their name. Now it's a chimney sweep or a miner. The painting of the black boy in satin was astonishing – I don't know where that is now. A lot of the time they just put them in the loft and get another one painted, or paint on top of it. I did manage to acquire one myself from a pub called The Arab Boy. They were changing the sign and I bought it. Eventually I got rid of it. That was a terrible painting. I've seen many variations of The Black Boy. Sadly, racist caricatures can be endlessly inventive.

TWR That reminds me of when, last summer, I was in Herne Bay in Kent. Two brutally stereo-typed wooden sculptures of black men had been placed at the entrance to one of the many junk shops on the high street. I heard the owner telling a customer that 'only one person has complained'. The customer said, 'People are so offended by everything these days, it's only history.'
IP That's just lazy thinking. History changes all the time. Those objects are historical, as are the pub signs, but this doesn't mean they don't exist in the present or won't in the future. Interestingly, though, the actual pub signs only last about ten years because they're exposed to the elements. The first one I saw looked pretty new, I'd say no more than five years old. It would have been painted in the 1970s. So that was their understanding of black people in the Seventies. But they're still painting these signs now. I've seen ones that look like Michael Jackson, and one recently of a North African guy with a Fez. Some are horrible racist caricatures and some are really amazing paintings, and you can see that they were done by a skilled artist, and the figure looks like it's based on a real human being. That's always very strange.

TWR One of the things you and I share is a love of folk songs. What draws you to this kind of music?
IP When I first moved out of my parents' house I lived with a woman who was an excellent singer, and she used to play the whistle. We would go to folk clubs a lot, in Cumbria and other places. It was a very white scene, but you'd find peculiar people at these clubs. There was a sense of history and heritage around that music that was evoked as singular, and something that didn't feel as though it included black people. But actually it does. The tunes travel and circulate among different folks, including black people in the US, for example, and come back in a slightly different form. We have Davey Graham, and people like Nadia Cattouse and Dorris Henderson, black female folk singers who have been forgotten.

Now you have folk music coming out of urban areas and it's not so linked to rural Britain and that narrow idea of history. It always felt like, where do I fit into that? But that's what I liked about it, that I could trace a mixture in a type of music that at the same time was definitively English. And there was also a sense of working-class identity that I felt I could connect to.

TWR Working-class identity seems equally as important to you as being black or queer or a woman. Your series *Working Images* (2008) was a really powerful exploration of this.
IP Yes, that series came about from when I was teaching and in residence at London South Bank University. The people in those photographs were non-academic staff at LSBU, the ones that allow the site to function day-to-day. I remember going to meet the people who did the sanitation and cleaning, and of course you had to get there at half past five in the morning when they were doing their work. It was interesting to talk to the students and see who actually spoke to any of these people. Some of them did, particularly to the catering staff and security team. Sometimes you'd see these figures quietly pushing their equipment around, and it was like nobody could see them, they were invisible.

The majority of security people were Nigerian, the cleaning staff were mostly from Latin America, the builders were typically English and Caribbean. I wanted to elevate them and acknowledge their contribution. The pictures I created were on a large scale and students had to pass them every day. The people in the photos were happy to be part of it. I met them all in their different gangs and told them about the project. Then a few from each group, be it security, or cleaning, or catering, self-selected to have their photo taken. I also included some of the media staff, the people who bring the projectors into the room and set things up.

TWR A lot of your work aims to take that invisible or unspoken figure and place them in the foreground. And that is celebratory, in a way...
IP I photograph a lot of shy, modest people. With *Pastoral Interlude* (1988), I wanted to take that easily overlooked figure and place them centrally within the frame. We're used to a certain, central image of rural England: rolling hills, etc. I wanted to use the black subject to interrupt this view so that the audience would look primarily at them, and then you can look behind and see a little bit of landscape. The landscape is always secondary, which subverts the stereotypical view of the English countryside.

TWR I recently read an anecdote about a farmer somewhere in rural England who was fined because he kept a messy farm, with rusty tractors and piles of rubbish. Tourists walking in the area complained because his mess was obscuring their anticipated, desired view of the landscape. The artist collective MyVillages talk about this as an example of the 'minor dictatorship' that rules over rural sites. Was the countryside also a place where you experienced the threat of being surveilled and policed in some way for not conforming?
IP I felt like I stood out; probably less so now, although I'm not so absolutely sure about that. It depends where you go. I've had people throw things, you know, stupid kids. That was a long time ago. And that hair-touching, when I used to have dreadlocks. I'd just see people coming towards me with their fingers outstretched ready to touch my hair. I used to go walking in the Lake District on my own, staying in a B&B. As a woman on your own, if someone's going to say something it's very scary, you don't have a friend to back you up. Sometimes I'd go walking and I wouldn't see anyone for an hour. I'd trip over and think, 'I could have broken my leg and nobody is around to help me.' There was a fear of people's reactions and what they're going to do, seeing me as an invader or something. That never really goes away. People just sort of pretend now. They hide it more. But those reactions, I felt, were never a reason not to go. It's their problem, not mine.

TWR Your series of photographic canvases *The Boy Who Watches Ships Go By* (2002) explores this sense of a figure who stands out, not just in relation to a particular landscape, but in relation to history: English history and also local history. The series does not directly represent this figure – a black boy who was supposedly buried at Sunderland Point, Lancashire, in 1739 – but instead reveals a selection of ghostly details of the location as it appeared over two centuries later. How did you discover this story?
IP I knew about the story before I visited Sunderland Point. It's near where [the artist and curator] Lubaina Himid lives, and she told me about it. The children of a local school choir used to sing a calypso song about the little black boy, 'Sambo'. So eventually I went to Sunderland Point and was told the official story of how the boy died there, longing for his captain. I thought that was a load of bollocks. When you go there it's weird, because at one point (in the eighteenth century) it would have been a teeming port and canal with ships coming in and passing through from the Caribbean, from Ireland, and other places. But now there's just a couple of fishermen and it's mainly tourists coming for the gravesite. It's humble fields, unconsecrated ground with cows grazing on it. I actually don't think there's anyone buried there. I saw the house where the boy is meant to have died, above the bakehouse. It's a spit of land that sticks out, so when the tide comes in it's cut off. So I imagined the boy waiting for the tide to come in, then waiting for it to go out.

Research for the piece led me to a ship's log, from a vessel that travelled to the Caribbean and back again. It was fantastic to see the language they'd used for illness, for the people who ran away, the endless weathers. They used to draw the way the land looked from the sea, so showing the shape of the cliffs rather than a bird's eye view map. They're all such beautifully painted documents. There are also letters from that time period. There was one that had been written after a ship had arrived in Gambia that was talking about cargo, and I wondered if they were talking about people. The documents are all there. It's a very strange site. On the shoreline there are pillars, fragments from a mansion, and a set of groins that stick up in the sea, all broken down. Little bits of evidence everywhere, but no cafés, no pubs. People just go there to visit the site, and then they go home again. It's very peculiar. Just across from there is where the Chinese cockle-pickers died in 2004. I got stuck in the mud there and I could see how dangerous it is.

TWR To me, your work has an agenda that can be described as 'decolonial', in the sense that you challenge the colonisation of history, of English history and the landscape in particular, by ideologies of nationalism and racism. Does the word 'decolonial' speak to you?

IP I don't like it. I don't think it's possible to 'decolonise'. It's a lazy word. I would never use it. With the idea of 'decolonising museums', for example, every context is different, be it the British Museum or a small regional museum. People have asked me to come and 'decolonise' their collection, and I say, 'I can imagine what I think you want me to do, but I can't decolonise.' That's at least a thirty-year job, starting with the relabelling of everything. It seems like an impossibly large task. But people talk about it as if it's a quick-fix, like you can get a load of black people to come in and look at it and it will all change. That would be a long, long job. The word doesn't seem to appreciate just how long colonisation took, how ingrained it still is and how the colonial mentalities are still around. So decolonising, it feels too easy. Like a catchphrase. So I'd never say that. I'd say exactly what I'm going to do.

TWR Do you have a favourite object inside your own home?

IP I have paintings and work by other artists that are important to me. They have their own histories and continue to delight me and support me. I also have a sculpture of a black child that I picked up at a reclamation yard. Strangely I felt like I rescued it/him.

C. G.-W.,
July 2020

WORKS

PLATES

XVI	from *Pastoral Interlude*, 1987
XVII	from *Pastoral Interlude*, 1987
XVIII	from *Near and Far*, 1998
XIX	from *Self Evident*, 1995
XX	from *Boy Who Watches Ships Go By*, 2002
XXI	*The Cost of the English Landscape*, 2018/1989
XXII	from *Working Images*, 2008
XXIII	from *Working Images*, 2008
XXIV	from *Oceans Apart*, 1991

"pastoral interlude"
... it's as if the Black experience is only lived within an urban environment.
I thought I liked the Lake District; where I wandered lonely as a Black face in
a sea of white. A visit to the countryside is always accompanied by a feeling
of unease; dread ...

... Searching for sea-shells; waves lap my wellington boots, carrying
lost souls of brothers & sisters released over the ship side ...

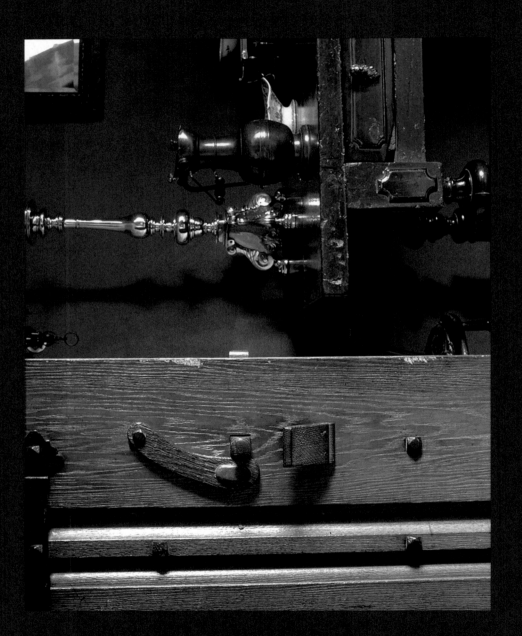

XVIII

XX

KEEP OUT

NO TRESPASS

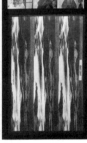

XXI

KEEP OUT

NO TRESPASS

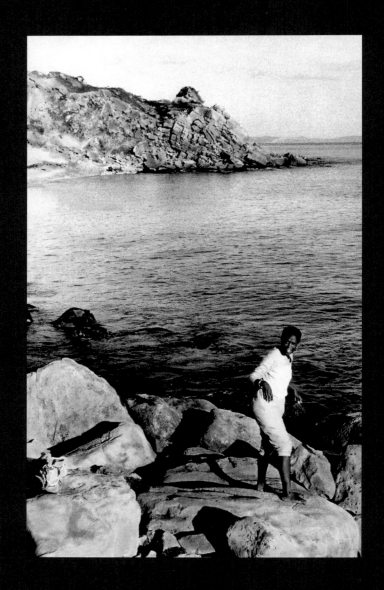

XXIV

JENNIFER LEE TSAI

POETRY

ABOUT CHINESE WOMEN

Suicide without a cause, or silent sacrifice for an apparent cause which,
in our age, is usually political: a woman can carry off such things without
tragedy, without even drama.
— Julia Kristeva

I

I return to a former self,
                               ghost or shadow self emerging from a glimmering light;

Woolf's 'luminous halo, a semi-transparent envelope surrounding us from the
beginning of consciousness to the end'

Life as circularity,
                       inevitable return to a womb-like space,
                                                                a space of the maternal?

Where do the dead go after they die? What nether region do they inhabit?

Where did the Hakka people come from? Peripatetic tribe from north-east
China.

She comes from people without a home, or fixed position. She is condemned
and doomed to wander looking for her place in history.

I conjure up the past, delving into the recesses of unknown memory and time.

I am returning to the source. The original source. The point of all our origin.
But these origins go further back beyond Western tradition, beyond the story
of holy innocence fabricated in the myths of Adam and Eve, and the notion
of a God the father. And it does not reside in the maternal womb either, that
place of warmth and nurturance, which begins with love.

I invite mystery. I return to our innate energy, excavating deeply layer upon
layer of our consciousness.

I breathe in the light; I inhale deeply and exhale...

Where is the point of our origin?

I am digging deep. I have to go further than the surface of things, back through space and time.

I uncover hidden treasure buried for centuries, and carefully retrieve it for future purposes.

Filtering through the coloured papers of memory, those delicate, fragile and carefully processed pieces of our past and history felt in my bones and body.

In the beginning there was the Word. And the Word is me. My words become me, and I become the word, a flurry of mixed phrases, half-spoken sentences, articulate in their gibberish.

I try to find the language that defines me, become a whirling dervish, caught up in a veil of spinning letters. They fly around me, and I try to catch them.

In the beginning there was the Word.

I am the signifier, the signified, signifying everything and nothing.

Once, I danced myself into a trance to find my grandmother's spirit.

When I felt it, my body shattered into tiny fragments.

Syncope – an absence of the self, time faltering, head spinning with a sudden vertigo.

Silent grandmother, guardian of secrets, please speak to me.

And when the repressed return to reclaim themselves, it will be terrifying.

II

A black-and-white family photograph taken in Hong Kong. The year is 1957 or 1958? My mother doesn't know exactly. There are three generations of *Hakka* people in the photograph – my grandparents and their children, my grandfather's brother and his family and my great-grandmother.

Hakka means guest families. They are nomadic migrants, renowned for their fortitude and resilience. In the nineteenth century, in clan wars against the Punti people, they built walled villages to protect themselves. My mother tells me how hard they worked all day in the fields growing rice, sweet potatoes, yams. There was no gas, no paraffin. They worked under the sun all day until it went dark. They sold their crops. The name of the area they lived in was Kuk Po. It was inhabited by seven clans – Sung (宋), Lee (李), Ho (何), Tsang (曾), Cheng (鄭), Ng (吳) and Yeung (楊). Today, Kuk Po is an abandoned village, inhabited by many ghosts. The town borders the Frontier Closed Area...

Three women sit in the middle of the photograph. In the centre, the matriarch – my great grandmother sits. In front of her, she parades her favourite grand-son, my uncle.
On her mother's lap, my mother is a toddler, looking at the camera with bewildered eyes.
My grandfather, who I hardly know, stands as a young, handsome man. My grandmother gazes at the camera with seemingly sad eyes but she is difficult to read. Is she angry, troubled, distrustful, resentful? What is it that flickers beneath the surface, caught in this singular moment?

I can see my aunt's features in my grandmother, her big, round eyes, her wide nose and full lips. All the women are dressed in dark clothes, the men in white shirts, the children in a mixture of traditional dress and Western clothes and what I find interesting about the photo is that the women are placed in the middle. No-one is smiling; even the children look sombre. It's as though some-one has died. And someone will die, two or three years after this photograph is taken – my grandmother. She will take her own life and leave her children behind. An eternal mystery; unreadable cipher. From generation to generation, an irretrievable grief, an irrevocable loss reverberates.

My mother will become motherless at the age of three or four, she will inherit a wicked stepmother but earn the guilt-stricken love of her grandmother trying to make amends for her sins. My mother tells me how her grandmother really loved her and saved an apple only for her every day. *No one else had an apple, only me.*

Mirror, Mirror on the wall. Who is the fairest of us all?

Do you remember her, Mammy? What was she like?

Like you, I remember many things from childhood. I can still remember seeing her foaming at the mouth after she drank the weed killer. I think she mustn't have drunk very much because she could still walk home back to the village. They tried to ferry her across the harbour to the city, but it was too late. Of course, she died.

Her body lies somewhere in an unmarked grave on the beach in San Tao. No one knows where she is buried. In recent years, my aunt bought a shrine for her in a cemetery in Hong Kong.

WOMAN WITH A WHITE PEKINGESE
ELIZABETH O'CONNOR

The women in her family have always shown dogs. They keep pictures of the dogs on the wall beside the staircase, a line-up in thick, bubble-like glass. The pictures are hung in a series of black oval frames. When she was a child she would look behind the sofa and through the hall door and see them there, hanging silently like a row of pinned beetles.

The pictures go back to sepia prints from the start of the last century, the first being her great-grandmother's prize-winning Pekingese, Cob. In these the dogs look athletic, their eyes small dark buttons. The pictures become gradually more detailed and colourful as they descend the stairs, ending in a series of young dogs that look like goblins, illustrations for a hallucinatory children's book.

Beneath each one her mother cuts out a small square of paper and tacks it to the wallpaper with gold pins. These squares document each dog's achievements. Damson's Best of Breed. Maggie's Best in Show. Deano, Agility Champion. Ugly Maura who never won anything but did once rescue a mouse from drowning in a rain-filled bucket.

The family's usual photographer is dead by the time she wants pictures of her own dog, Marie. She has to find a new one on the internet, on a website whose landing page is shaped like an unfurled scroll. The cursor becomes a white quill and the photographer's name is scrawled out in an animation at the top of the page.

He has a studio above a stationery shop in the centre of her town, and wears double-lensed glasses that make his eyes spill across his face. He calls the dogs things like 'arrogant' and 'stately' and chews the edges of his fingernails to scabs.

He pulls down a screen over a metal set of drawers and the dogs sit in front of it. The first screen depicts a pink sky and white clouds, and he tries others: a castle on a hill, a rainbow, plain colours, dark so that the subject stands out like in an oil painting. She doesn't get a say in Marie's background: he gives her a Japanese garden. His camera has a long orange feather pinned to the top, so that Marie stays still watching it. Then he brings out other feathers, blue and green, which he presents like a bunch of flowers to make Marie look slightly left, slightly right.

In the final picture, Marie looks over to the left. The dog's pure white fur brings out colours that gently move behind the glass. Peach, pink, pear-green. Once it is hung, she likes to think that Marie was looking at something on the wall, something no one else could see.

*

12.00 p.m.

She remembers the photographer while she's eating noodles in the arena cafeteria. She has decided that this year's dog show would be her last and is surprised by the relief she feels. The noodles are congealing in their polystyrene container and Marie whines and paws at her leg. The man behind the counter looks very tired and keeps splattering mashed potato on himself as he serves it. A couple at the table next to her, both in formal pink shirts and blue jeans, argue in furtive voices.

She picks out a few strands of noodle and a piece of carrot and drops them to the floor, and Marie falls quiet.

Why oh why would you call him your great love though –

Because he is —

How is he —

He's helped me through some very —

Baby, baby he's a dog —

Under the table a small white face lowers onto two paws. She starts for a second, wonders if Marie has got loose, before realising it's another dog, whose fur curls tight against its skin, rather than hanging in a fringe like Marie's.

There's a hollow knocking on the Pyrex window next to her, and a face she recognises. Ella always wears frosted pink lipstick that makes her teeth look especially yellow, but she smiles widely and her voice has a quality that makes dogs look instantly up at her with fondness. Marie recognises the face too, and pulls her out of the cafeteria to greet it.

Ella squeals when she sees them both. She pulls her in for a hug, smelling of Yves Saint Laurent Paris. She has a poodle, Belle, silver and black. Belle tugs on the lead as she gets close to Marie, her sleek body suddenly inelegant and desperate. The two dogs sniff at one another. Belle becomes fixated on a piece of noodle stuck in Marie's leg fur.

I think she can smell something, Cath.

Just cafeteria smell, probably.

Oh.

How are you?

Fine, Cath. Have you been placed today?

Not yet. You?

Best Bitch.

I'll say.

Funny. Saw David around the stalls.

Did you?

Oh yes. Is he well?

Yes. Very well. Your husband?

Fine.

Belle rolls over onto her back, crushing the elaborate pom–pom of hair on her shoulders.

Belle, no. No, Belle. Belle, stop.

I don't think she understands.

She does. She does. Look at her ears, she's listening. Belle, please could y—

An announcement on the speakers. Mostly crackle.

A photographer walks past and snaps a series of Belle and Marie, making clucking sounds to get them to look at the camera. He does not even glance at the two women.

*

In a doctor's waiting room, she reads an article about sea-wolves in British Columbia. She reads that they were once normal wolves, but had evolved over centuries to live on beaches and coasts, rather than on plains and in forests. They are remarkable swimmers, as a result, and possess a unique intelligence honed from having to find ways to crack the shells of shore-creatures and judge the moving of the tide. There are glossy pictures of them, sleek between the currents of the sea. Over a double-page spread is a photo of the pack on the beach. One has its paw up over an orange crab, its claws held defensively in the air. Another shoves its snout into a wig of seaweed. One stares at the camera directly, its grey fur gleaming amber against the sea. In the background, on the cliff that swings around the left of the photograph, a hulking black bear cowers against an ash tree.

When she gets home she remembers the article as she forks mackerel into Marie's food bowl, the smell of salt and brine lingering in the kitchen. Marie looks up at her with an expression of complete desperation, like her organs will fail if she doesn't put the bowl on the floor.

Every time she thinks about it she hears the cracking of the shells between the wolves' teeth, their heads bowed to clean out the soft flesh, and she gets a thought in her brain that she should open the nearest window and throw Marie straight out of it.

*

12.25 p.m.

She combs Marie's hair, keeps finding drops of noodle broth staining it pale yellow. She gets the stain out by running oil over it and rubbing it between her fingers. Marie thinks she is playing and snaps at her.

Marie is the only white Pekingese she has ever seen that isn't Albino. When Marie is born she has a double-page spread in the London Reform Pekingese Club newsletter, a tiny pale seal-pup-thing cupped in her hands. She is described as The Future. When she gets the pictures back, she is shocked at how ancient her hands look in comparison to Marie's body, how ungodly and unpure are her dirty fingernails.

She has been assigned a large pink box in the centre of the arena. The boxes are lined up in a grid formation, each one given to a dog and their handler. When she arrived, a young woman gave her a pink ticket and sent her here. The dogs are supposed to sit inside the box, so that it acts like a den or cave, keeping them calm. She has a small fold-out table for Marie to sit on, one of her husband's jump-ers draped over the top, and she joins Marie in the box herself. Sitting there keeps her calm more than it does Marie, she admits.

A man stops near their box while she is standing and grooming Marie. He moves unnaturally, fiddling with his phone. She sees him tilt his body in a way that suggests he's taking a picture of Marie.

Excuse me?

Is this Maura?

The man licks his lips, leaving a thin layer of saliva.

No. This is her daughter.

She's a real winner.

I hope so.

My wife always loved Maura. Always a shame she never —

She stops listening, pulls a hairclip from her hair and piles a layer of Marie's fur on top of the dog's head. She starts brushing out the underlayers, pressing them back on themselves so that they lift. The man looks at her quizzically, as though he has just asked a question. She notices the green rosette on his jumper, a low-status winner of the Utility group. His dog, a Bedlington terrier, gazes forlornly up at him.

Did you know that? Bedlingtons used to hunt rats in mines. They still could, if they wanted to.

He bends and ruffles the bobble of curly fur atop the dog's head.

May I take a picture? My wife loves Pekingese. And a white one. Phew!

Okay.

He takes a few and looks at her. His mouth twitches.

What?

Could you... Not be in the picture?

She steps aside, her comb upright in her hand. Heat rises to her face.

*

1.05 p.m.

A message on the Tannoy echoes through the arena.

Pekingese, Ring 5.

She is holding up a pocket mirror, applying lipstick and backcombing her hair into waves. Marie is sleeping.

The linoleum is pea-green and magnifies the pattering sound of the dogs' claws and short legs. She scratches the inside of her palm with the long nail on her ring finger. Her favourite shade of pink, already chipped.

Opposite her, a woman massages the back of her Skye terrier. She wears a hoodie bearing a close-up of the dog's face. She recognises her. At one of her first shows the woman had bought her a jacket potato from the cafeteria. The woman never won anything, but she came back every year. Once she had said to her, if I had only one wish, I'd wish that my dog could speak to me.

Her shoulder is knocked by someone walking towards Ring 5. She looks out and says Excuse me, but the figure walks by. Someone in a grey suit. Her eyes follow the lead down to the small animal shuffling beside him.

Another Pekingese, white as Marie. Perhaps whiter.

Her phone buzzes in her pocket. Her mother.

Cath,,

She looks up and the white dog is gone. She waits for the next message to come through.

Cath – don't 4get 2 carry cubes of cheese. xx

Her mother had been the one to discover her way of training: coaxing dogs into doing certain actions with food. Cheese was best, although mackerel or carrots were also popular. Pieces of boiled egg, too, though these made her pockets smell.

She rushes a message back.

Have u heard of another white Pekingese? One is here this year. X

She presses send and some primal feeling sparks off in her stomach, making her want to run.

*

When she is at school, she reads a long poem about a man who leaves his home to go to sea, and only comes back decades later. His dog is the only thing to recognise him. Of course, she thinks.

*

1.15 p.m.

The ring is on the other side of the vast arena hall. The sounds of the crowd echo into the curved, iron-beamed roof, which reminds her of the rib cage of some fantastic creature. She sees the other white Pekingese again, glimpses it between the legs of some children, in the gaps between another row of pink boxes. A train of dachshunds weaves through the space in front of her. She hears the owner say to a bystander that the breed used to hunt rats in Bavaria. She sees the white Pekingese again and follows it so closely she almost walks into a woman in a green knitted cardigan, cradling her Dalmatian like a giant baby.

The woman spots her looking as she walks on. He's having a rest, she mutters.

*

Her husband buys her Maura, Marie's mother, with the money from his first book advance. He trusses up an old cardboard box with tissue paper and ribbon and leaves it on the kitchen table. When she enters the room he plunges his hands inside and pulls out Maura, her tiny black paws whirring like bicycle pedals.

When she first meets her husband, in a bar by the canal in the centre of town, he lights up when she mentions her family's dogs. He calls her his show pony, his best in show. She decides not to tell him about the rest, the hours of waiting, the house in the middle of nowhere so the dogs could run free, the years scheduled by the dogs' mating, the smell of dog shampoo in a tin bath, the way a dog penis feels when it rubs against your bare teenage leg.

Maura is pure toffee-coloured, her fur sitting thick on her head like a bonnet. When she finally decides to show her, Maura loses: according to the judges she is bow-legged and has an incorrect wedge-shaped head. She has bought a new outfit for the occasion, a red tweed suit and a silk shirt, the most expensive thing she has ever owned. She never wears it again.

*

1.30 p.m.

She knows that look. They've all perfected it. Darling, I'm so happy for you. So happy I could just knock my teeth out with a hammer. So happy I could climb into a coffin and slam it shut!

There are gigantic screens erected over the top of the stands around the arena seating, and this same face is everywhere. The judging for American cocker spaniels is finishing and the winner, a tri-colour with an ugly swollen head, sneezes constantly as it is placed on the podium. As the camera zooms in on its hazel eyes the animal turns, filling the shot with auburn and black hair.

She strains to catch a glimpse of the other white Pekingese. Every flash of white in her vision causes her to jerk involuntarily towards it. And because she's looking, suddenly everything seems white. Teeth, shirt collars, pearl necklaces, old people hair, dandruff.

The man in front of her turns and watches her, asks if he looks nervous.
She says, No.
Marie stands up on her back legs, her pink tongue curling up towards her teeth.

*

When her mother first begins dying, she asks her daughter to go and buy her a sleep robot. In the shop the sales assistant looks sympathetically at her and leads her to a row of what look like grey stones. They have speakers attached, she sees when she gets close. The assistant explains that they play sounds to lull the listener to sleep: rain, tide, heartbeat, breathing.

*

The more I meet people, the more I love my DOG. Her mother has a cap with this emblazoned on it in silver felt.

*

1.58 p.m.

The judge's jacket reminds her of the wallpaper at her mother's house, turquoise and cream stripes. She walks around the green linoleum of the arena and feels her shoes squeak. She looks for her husband in the audience, the stage lights reflecting off his pink head. Most of the seats are empty, dark like the gap of a tooth.

The lead is thin and wiry, and each time Marie breathes it sends movement up to her hand. She can judge Marie's mood this way, whether she can run faster than normal or is going to be stubborn. The knowledge is something she has always had. Her husband liked to tell people about it at parties, as though she had some secret talent. Often men would scoff back to him that she was projecting and couldn't tell a thing. Then her husband would say, I suppose that is true.

She waits in silence as the judge runs his hands over another Pekingese, chocolate-coloured, moving its legs like a wooden doll. The Pekingese seems perturbed by the act, craning its neck back to sniff the judge's hand.

In the stalls she sees a small white face emerge, followed by a slug-like body. She looks hard, wanting to recognise the dog's owner, but the light changes, suddenly, and they fall in shadow. She hears clapping.

The judge walks toward her, smiling, extending his hand, and she feels the lead in her hand jerk as Marie instinctively begins to move forward. The judge's hand feels dry and tight, like the hand of a ghost, and he pins a red rosette to the lapel of her jacket. She wonders if he does this to everyone, even the men, but he is walking away again now and the audience are starting to leave. The man who asked if he looked nervous is talking to her, asking for Marie's pedigree name. Her feet on the ground feel sure and solid, like walking on a thick path of snow.

*

Her mother watches television in bed. Her mother doesn't live at home any more, but she picks a black dog hair from the cream bedsheets, finds a small brown whisker embedded in the carpet, things her mother must have carried with her somehow.

The two of them curl up under the covers and they watch her mother's favourite video on the television at the end of the bed, an old recorded live performance of a man with various puppets. He stands in front of a velvet curtain, baby blue, the light pricking the silver of the microphone into white. (He died the same month as her father, which they both know but do not mention.) The man's puppets are a gangly monkey and a giant baby bird. Each one talks to him with great intimacy, as though they are in league against the audience.

Do you know why I like this? her mother says, morphine softening her body to butter. Those puppets talk to him like the dogs used to talk to me.

She turns and says, What? But her mother is already asleep.

*

2.08 p.m.

A mother and son approach her as she combs out Marie's fur again. The child is sweet-looking, with a shock of black hair and freckles. The mother speaks softly, asks if her child can ask her a question. She nods. The boy points to Marie, and says, Does she think that she is human, or does she think that you're a dog?

She thinks of Marie in the park, whining to go home. Marie proud on the kitchen tiles, the headless body of a mouse at her feet. Marie barking and growling at a cat that came too close to the house. Marie sneezing and play-fighting with her hands, a language she cannot decipher but that makes her feel at home in the world. She tells the boy, Both.

*

2.42 p.m.

She sits waiting for the next announcement, for the decision of Best of Breed to be made. The title is between Marie and a black male Pekingese named Fuwari, full name Fuwari Yoshikawa Find Me on the Mountainside Denbo. Fuwari's owner feeds cat-shaped treats to Marie and makes kissing noises, stroking her head and singing in a language she doesn't understand. Fuwari stays close to his owner, and she is surprised by how rejected she feels.

*

About a month after Maura had her first litter, she died. An infection in the womb. The puppies were old enough to survive, luckily, and her mother's dog, a bullish silver Pekingese named Tyrell, became their stern role-model. Tyrell played with them, disciplined them, but refused to sleep with them, and she didn't want to sleep with the puppies herself in case she rolled over and crushed them during the night. But if the puppies were left alone, they would grow too anxious and begin to eat each other. So she wrapped a towel around a hot water bottle and a ticking clock, and placed that in their basket. The puppies slept, and when she took it away in the morning they held onto the towel with their teeth, and whined for hours.

On her first day in the hospice her mother says, I know how those puppies feel now. I know how Maura must have felt too.

*

3.15 p.m.

She phones her mother outside the venue, where a group of pigeons have descended on an open bag of crisps. She tells her about Marie winning her group, about Fuwari's owner shaking her hand with tears in his eyes. Her mother congratulates her and she feels still for a moment, despite Marie pulling hard on her lead to be nearer to the birds.

How is St Mary's? she asks.
It's good. Daffodils are out. The foxes come out at night.
How are you feeling?
Fine.
Her mother breathes out heavily.
I'm glad Callie did so well.

*

Congratulations!
Thank you.
So pleased for you.
Thank you.
You'll be competing in the Toy final?
Yes.
And who knows from there.
Yes!
Beautiful coat.
Thank you.
Really lovely.
Thank you.
Your mother is here?
Yes.
And your husband?
Yes. Yes.

*

She is eight and Callie is eighteen months and she trains the dog before school, using black pudding. Callie has endless attention. They spend an hour in the field behind the house sitting and standing, sitting and standing. The rain drizzling and the light licking at them. It is a fine art. She imagines taking Callie to agility trials and winning, to a movie audition and winning. Training Callie makes her feel good, makes her think, I am good. Callie trails her to school like a guard dog, sleeps at the foot of her bed. At night she dreams of Callie growing wings and flying her across the night sky, the rivers winding below like thread.

*

3.45 p.m.

She wants coffee. She can smell it – vaguely – beneath the usual dog-show smell of dog and hairspray, and deserves it with sugar for winning.

She walks by a glamorous woman in a pink suit, holding a microphone with a spongy yellow top. She stares and trips over her own feet, for which the women shoots her a hard glare. She notices the woman has terrible eyeliner on, a black line going around her whole eye like a zero that makes her look mad and terrified.

You were in the shot then.

Sorry. My dog pulled me.

Not very good behaviour.

Are you talking about me or my dog?

The woman turns away, flicks her fringe out of her eyes ready for another take. The man behind the camera waves his hand and the woman starts talking with a wide smile.

She realises she is still in shot and slowly edges out of it, then turns and carries on walking. She walks by a stand selling swaddling mats for dogs, another selling tiny hair-straighteners. The man on the stand spots Marie first, her waddling mass of wild hair, and tries to catch her eye.

Don't, she says.

*

It is winter and Callie trails her to school like a pale shadow. She loses sight of her, sometimes, until her docked tail appears above a series of low shrubs, or she bounds out of the trees. The snow muffles the sound of her calls and so she devises a series of hand movements for when Callie is in her line of vision, a flick of her wrist for Stay, or waving her hand in a shooing motion for Go.

She reads that dogs can see the earth's magnetic field, which she imagines in her head like a haze of blue on the ground. She wonders how her movements look against it, if her limbs blur into it like a long-exposure photograph, if Callie can truly tell her apart from anything else that resembles her in any way.

*

4.20 p.m.

She drinks her coffee while sitting in the pink box, Marie sleeping on the table in front of her. The coffee burns her tongue raw with the first sip. She thinks that someone has stolen one of her hairclips and scans the crowd for it, a flash of silver.

The St. Bernard occupying the box next to her has returned from the ring and sits on the floor, his cavernous head resting against her thigh. He rolls out his tongue from the side of his jaw, his loose jowls leaving a smear of spittle against the pink wool of her trousers. She pushes him off. A wet string of saliva remains suspended between them.

She looks up at the dog's owner, expecting an apology.

He likes you, says the owner, smiling.

*

5.00 p.m.

She doesn't see the white Pekingese again until after the Toy Group judging. This takes place in a bigger ring than the first and is busier, with one dog from each breed in the group and their handlers. Some of them even have fans, like a tiny fawn-coloured Chihuahua followed by a gaggle of children and cameras. She bends down and caresses the inner down of Marie's ear, and Marie leans into her hand.

The competitors are lined up behind a green curtain, waiting to be called out onto the arena stage. It is dark and filled with the sound of dogs panting.

The woman behind her brushes her terrier's coat so that it fans out around the dog's body. She brushes it until it shines heavenly, like the inside of a shell.

She is called to run around the edge of the ring by a young man in black, who has a headset glued to his ear. He mumbles something and pushes his hand hard against her shoulder, makes some gestures to someone or something at the other side of the ring. He nods, and pulls the curtain to one side, pushing her beyond it.

The curtain has fallen over Marie, who couldn't pass through it fast enough. She stoops down and fixes the dog's hair, and Marie jumps up a little. She sees that the floor is scattered with flecks of black material, leftovers from the police dogs' demonstration. She had watched on one of the screens as a group of offi-cers set the dogs on a man dressed as a burglar, while 'Bad Boys' played overhead.

The other breeds follow her. Three variations of hairless breeds. Two kinds of Chihuahua. A barrel-like pug at the back, who she can hear snorting. A Maltese, whose feet walk so fast under such long hair the dog looks like it is floating.

A man's voice announces each breed and the audience claps and cheers. All the handlers pull combs from their pockets and brush out the dogs' coats, moving their paws so that each animal stands in a specific, identical way, with its head tilted upwards and its feet set back.

She doesn't recognise the judge, a thin man in a three-piece maroon suit. She smiles at him and he remains blank. He motions for her to start her performance.

She feels the weight of eyes on her as she notices the television cameras at the edges of the ring. She has perfected this way of walking: slow enough for Marie's short legs to keep up, quick enough to let the air ripple through her long fur, making it bounce and catch the light.

She watches the judge at the far end of the ring. He nods, writes something down. She knows that nod. It's good. Her heart surges forward. She sees a woman at the front of the crowd, clapping passionately as Marie walks.

The lead suddenly tugs at her hand. Her smile falters. Marie has decided she wants to sit down. The judge looks up, cuts her down with his glare. She pulls the lead gently, smiles faux-sheepishly. What can you do? Charming. Pekingese are expected to have character. Titters in the audience. Marie going nowhere. She pulls the lead again, harder this time. Marie adjusts her legs, sits down more fully. She pulls again. Hard. She hears the yelp from deep in Marie's throat. She hears it echo across the floor.

*

She wonders if her husband will watch her on the TV. She looks for him in the audience, in the crowds. Ella said she had seen him. He used to come to the shows every year. He would watch her perform and bring her a milky coffee afterwards. In recent years he has not paid attention as he once did: his face lit blue by the phone in his lap, the coffee forgotten. Still, she had thought she might see him today. She thinks of him watching at home instead, a glimpse of her appearing between the agility trials and a segment on organic dog food. He sits on a sofa she can't imagine, in a room she has never seen.

It has only been a week since he moved out. That was not the surprising bit. The surprising bit was when she presented him with an idea for how they could split custody of Marie, a spreadsheet she'd made and printed off (with Clip Art to keep the tone friendly) and he said, Actually I'm not bothered at all. Keep her.

*

6.00 p.m.

She cries in the car park. It is her last dog show and she really, truly expected to win.

*

It is winter and Callie trails her to school like a pale shadow. The woods are out of bounds after someone died there, buried in a heap of snow, so she follows the road, the car lights amber and red against the dark. She practises their hand movements. Flicking her wrist, Stay. Moving her hand in a shooing motion, Go. She is distracted by something. She can never remember what. A squirrel or a hunk of snow falling from a branch. She puts her hand up instinctively, and Callie follows her order by running into the road.

*

7.00 p.m.

The routes out of the arena car park lead immediately to the countryside, where the paths are dark and winding. She sees dark shapes at the edges of the road but cannot make out what they are.

*

The man with blood on his hands asks her angrily if the dog is hers. She looks down as Callie's eyes roll in her head, as something dark grows over the pit of her stomach.

No, she says. I've never seen it before.

*

She and her mother play a game at dog shows. They ask a handler for every breed how they would describe their dog's temperament. They get a point every time the handler says 'loyal', 'intelligent', or 'characterful'. They get ten points if the handler says 'loves everything and everyone'. They end up with so many points each that the game becomes boring. The game becomes to find a single owner who doesn't say any of those things.

*

8.05 p.m.

The last time she sees it is in the motorway service station, when she is deciding between a strawberry and a chocolate milkshake. The white Pekingese shuffles out of the toilets with its owner. The owner is a kind-looking young man, a teenager with red spots covering his chin and a lot of hair gel. He carries a brown paper bag with grease staining the bottom. She waves to him, points to

Marie and then to his own dog. He smiles awkwardly at her.

She follows him into the car park. She wants to ask who the breeder is, whether there were other white Pekingese in the litter. Part of her thinks she can offer advice, too. She remembers being that age, attending the dog shows, the youngest person competing by decades.

He looks over his shoulder, spots her and speeds up. She realises she is speeding up too, her walk becoming a rigid trot. His dog sees Marie and jerks him backwards, but he carries on moving. He pulls open his car boot, bundles the dog inside and walks over to the passenger seat.

The car leaves, the top of the white dog's head bobbing in the back window.

She looks at the sky, streaked dark. The clouds are lit from within. She thinks they look sort of like bones.

*

8.27 p.m.

Her phone buzzes. A message from her husband, something about returning a suitcase.

*

8.53 p.m.

On the car radio, she hears a name she recognises. The man with the puppets, and the baby blue curtain. One year since he died. They announce an auction of the puppet collection. She thinks suddenly that she should buy one, could present it to her mother as a surprise. Then the price: a small house deposit, years of holidays, most of what she earns in a year.

Then she thinks about how the puppets are probably still full of him, his dead skin cells forever jammed in the folds of each puppet's body, pieces of his fingernails and his palms, scabs from where he might have cut himself in the garden or peeling potatoes, knuckle hair. The thought makes her shudder.

They play a clip of one of his shows, one she recognises. In her head she delivers the punchline a beat before he does.

*

9.15 p.m.

She stops to have a cigarette at the edge of the motorway. Marie sniffs around in the undergrowth. They are standing at the edge of a field which slopes down to a section of marshland below. In the marshland is a dark pool broken by islands of mud and grass.

The light is dying and the lights of the cars shimmer hazily. The traffic seems to be slowing down up ahead as though deadened by congestion. Marie digs at something under the wet leaves, then suddenly stops and looks forward, every muscle in her small body tense and alert. She thinks about climbing into the car and leaving her there, how long it would take Marie to notice she had gone. A shape moves in the corner of her eye.

Four white egrets stand in the marsh. One bends and its neck shuttles down something from the water, a mudskipper or beetle. One scratches at the space between its wing and its breast. Another shakes out its feathers, like a dog emerging from a pool. The last one stands still.

Marie emits a quiet bark.

The four birds take flight, their legs trailing behind them. She thinks that she'll be able to see where they go, four white shapes against the dark trees, but they disappear quickly, into thin air.

*

She shows a middle-aged couple around her mother's house. She tells them about the litters of puppies she has raised there, and the couple laugh and coo. She doesn't let them look under the stairs, where the dogs were all born, because shit has stained the skirting board a dank orange.

*

9.23 p.m.

Marie is in the front seat. She rests her snout on her feet, and falls asleep.

Her phone shows a message from her mother, asking about the show.

*

9.44 p.m.

Another message from her mother, this time about Callie and has Cath seen her? And when will Cath be home from school?

*

10.20 p.m.

A missed call from St Mary's.

The traffic is slow and the car is still.

She closes her eyes and listens to the rain pile up against the window. She wonders if the storm will pass before she has opened them.

*

Here is the dream she has. She returns from holiday in winter. The field behind her house is covered in snow. Her nose runs and she can feel it slowly turning to ice above her lip. The windows in the house are dark and she knows instinctively that it is empty, colder inside than it is here. She gets closer and realises that the snow is moving, that the land is really the body of a thousand dogs, all sleeping dogs waking up to the sounds of her footsteps. She snaps twigs under her feet and her mouth erupts in steam. Each breath wakes up a new dog from the earth. They shake their fur and underneath they are white. The air is filled with whining, with barking, with the ground snapping at her heels.

She feels herself being pulled downwards. They are so happy to see her.

INTERVIEW   FANNY HOWE

Fanny Howe's bibliography is as bewildering as her itinerant biography. Born in 1940 in Buffalo, New York, the poet and author grew up in Cambridge, Massachusetts, before moving an estimated thirty times in six decades – spiralling around New York, Massachusetts and California states, with volleys to Ireland, where her talented mother, Mary Manning, was born and raised – only to settle back in Cambridge in her seventies. Howe's books, all fifty (at least) of them, track these moves: as she suggests in this interview, place informs her writing 'completely, like being dropped in water. It is the environment.' With a majority of her books – published by independent and experimental presses – out of print, to be a reader of Fanny Howe is to be a seeker.

   '[T]he greatest writer there is,' wrote Eileen Myles of Howe, who has, however, eschewed fame. Her humility is active, her obscurity intentional. She rarely grants interviews and undermines the authority others might claim given her talents and family. A 'long-tailed' Bostonian, '[s]he can trace her lineage back to the *Mayflower*,' wrote her daughter, acclaimed author Danzy Senna (whose husband, Percival Everett, was interviewed in *The White Review* No. 28), of Fanny, whose father was a Harvard professor and a civil rights lawyer and mother a playwright and film pioneer. Samuel Beckett was a family friend of her mother. Susan Howe, Fanny's older sister, is as renowned for her poetry as are *her* children for their art: R. H. Quaytman, painting, and Mark von Schlegell, science fiction.

   Though Fanny Howe inherited wealths of history, politics, art and culture, such privileges and responsibilities came with neither money nor property. 'There were many women like me,' she reflects in *The Wedding Dress: Meditations on Word and Life* (University of California Press, 2003), 'born into white privilege but with no financial security, given a good education but no training for survival.' In essays, Howe stories the difficulties of raising three children alone – divorced from their father, the Black American writer Carl Senna – in a nation defined by the violent exploitation of minorities. Through teaching, community work and writing, Howe has worked with thorough, subtle care on behalf of the vulnerable in America. Ariana Reines called Howe's latest book – *Night Philosophy* (Divided Publishing, 2020) – 'a manual for surviving evil'.

   Howe's writing is formally precise, poetry even when it's prose. Philosophical, mythic, mystic and religious. The author is a converted, practising Catholic of the Liberation Theology kind that is Marxist – wherein good Catholics are radical activists and obscurity is a means to truth, beauty, and justice, like doubt to God. This interview – at times aphoristic, conversational, informational – was conducted over the course of six months, first via email and in person, beginning in February 2020 in Greenwich Village, then continuing via Zoom and more emails during the Covid-19 lockdown. I had met Fanny Howe once before. In October 2018, I travelled to her apartment in Cambridge to film her reading from a favourite book. She selected *A Tomb for Anatole* by Stéphane Mallarmé (translated by Paul Auster), pieces composed after the death of the poet's eight-year-old son. Dimly lit and painted far off-white with round wooden arches and religious art on the walls, her apartment looks like a church backroom. Framed family photographs line the kitchen, where tea is offered. Howe chose to read in her bedroom, beside a wide, horizontally inclined window like the glass casket of Snow White (her reference). In the footage, the book glows in her hands. She is tiny in the chair.   FIONA ALISON DUNCAN

THE WHITE REVIEW Has anyone approached you about writing your biography?
FANNY HOWE No. I feel my five novels in *Radical Love* are close enough.

TWR Who, besides you, knows your biography best?
FH Probably my younger sister, Helen, and my children.

TWR What sense of privacy do you desire for yourself?
FH Eighty per cent.

TWR Could you qualify that quantity?
FH I only like to spend about two hours a day with people.

TWR How was that with having three children?
FH Children are easy compared with grown-ups.

TWR Your book *Night Philosophy* includes several texts that weren't written by you but could have been, for example the United Nations' 1959 'Declaration of the Rights of the Child', which you re-title 'The Rights of the Child (UN) Known Only to Adults'. On first read, I thought you'd authored that document. With lines like 'The child shall have the right to adequate nutrition, housing, recreation and medical services', it reads like fiction, since we aren't abiding by it at all, or not in the United States at least.
FH Not at all. I know. The whole of that book was sort of like an embryonic unfolding. I had no real plan for it. In a sense I just wanted to see more clearly. I hoped to discover one idea that ran through all of my work, and if it showed I was finished. It was sort of a recapitulation with the purpose of seeing what was there, what I had apparently cared about twenty or thirty years ago. Did I still care? Was I the same person? Do thoughts make the person? I have never used the technique of cross-referencing or sampling, but I see, in the juxtaposition of two or three texts, a disruption in the tone and textures of each one. But they do not carry irony, just a strangeness, an echo. Among those were the little quote from G.K. Chesterton and the long quote from Michel de Certeau which appear in the book, and which elucidated a central idea.

TWR What's that idea?
FH It involves a kind of person who is at the

mercy of the developing world, who can't quite figure out how to manage. This world now is made for might and ownership. I think you recognise in childhood the strategies that are necessary for being alone or adapting to surroundings, whatever they are. One example being how you go through school, from elementary, to middle, to high, to college, to a job, and you have to be somehow able to figure all that out, the timing and what you have to do to get to the next step. All this takes an understanding of the world based on ancient customs of domination and territory. There are people wandering around who don't get it, and that includes many who are very intelligent. I think women have figured out strategies to disarm men, but it has not allowed them time to think of what it has cost.

TWR I was wondering if you've seen any Hayao Miyazaki films, like *Howl's Moving Castle* or *Spirited Away*? They have child protagonists, too, but Miyazaki's characters *always* 'figure it out' with grace.
FH Yes, I love those films. I loved *Spirited Away*, that might be my favourite.

TWR With the figure you're describing, is theirs a nonviolent position?
FH It tends towards nonviolence: they would rather run away than get killed. [Laughs.] There aren't only two ways, killing or being killed; you can also collaborate, run away, signal and hide. There are people who can compete and other people who get frightened or confused. There was an idea of poets into the 1950s that they would lie in bed drinking, shooting up and writing poems. And why not? There's a narrow trail between wonder and competence.

TWR I see this figure in many of your texts. It could be the voice of this poem from *O'Clock* (Reality Street Editions, 1995): 'Scared stiff and fairy-struck / Under the oak tree / Under the moon – pink hawthorne / By a stony well – very sacred, / Very stuff.' It could be the bewildered mother in *Saving History* (Sun & Moon Classics, 1998). The heroine of *Bronte Wilde* (Reality Street Editions, 2020, originally published with Avon Books, 1976). I wondered if Dzhokhar and Tamerlan Tsarnaev, the brothers who bombed the Boston Marathon, as you write about them in *The Needle's Eye* (Graywolf Press, 2016), could be it?

And *Nod* (Sun & Moon Books, 1998), of course, begins: 'Between a children's progress from a heavenly world to a world that is a likeness of heaven and then to a world which is delivered and upheld by a dream of heaven, there is only the world.' Are my examples just?

FH Yes. My short poems collected in *O'Clock* were written in Ireland. They condense many of the thoughts I had already had and was going to have more of. It helped to be away from America to make them float off-kilter, like translations almost. I don't think I have written a book without a child in it. I think this follows my feeling about human development from conception on, the stages that are composed of disappearance, replacement, as if there were a figure being made, a potential in process.

TWR *Bewilderment* is a word and concept that repeats in your work. This is from a talk you gave in 1998 [later published in *The Wedding Dress: Meditations on Word and Life*]: 'Bewilderment is an enchantment that follows a complete collapse of reference and reconcilability. It cracks open the dialectic and sees myriads all at once. The old debate over beauty – between absolute and relative – is ruined by this experience of being completely lost by choice! [...] Bewilderment circumambulates, believing that at the centre of errant or circular movement, is the axis of reality.' Is bewilderment the experience of the recurring figure in your work?

FH *Bewilderment* is the result of a ton of reading in various texts and traditions, and I think I was feeling defiant because of the crushing sense of failure I carry with me. I decided to stand up for the weakness of it all.

TWR In that same talk you propose 'Bewilderment as a poetics and an ethics'. Regarding ethics, bewilderment's vastness of perspective, decentring the ego, seems conducive both to writing poetry and to caretaking, reducing harm. I wonder if there's another way to think about your central figure, as vulnerable, yes, but far from ignorant ('lost by choice!'). If dumbfounded, what they don't get is *why* customs of domination and territory are demanded of them in order to 'achieve'.

FH There's always some concealed social type you are meant to be. Psychoanalysis, religion, manners, business... each and all have a model of achievement. If you can keep your objectivity, it *is* interesting to see how these things work either from the bottom or the middle, the amount of lying and self-deception that's involved. Someone did a study of poets, and most of them who are doing well now went to good universities and grew up with money – inherited money. But no one would dare have a conversation about that. White, white. Whiteness now has the pallor of cowardice. That whiteness quotient was hard to miss. Good fortune is the subject of fiction over centuries, and its connection to a culture – look at Dickens. By culture I mean production, the gathering of people around a central value, to produce it more efficiently and safely. Privilege is the guarantee of blindness to your own conformism.

TWR I saw you've been attending Black Lives Matter protests this summer. How has that experience been for you, and how has it connected to your past experiences with the Civil Rights Movement? You worked for CORE (Congress of Racial Equality), for instance, and your father was a civil rights lawyer.

FH The great thing is to live long enough to see the return of values and people in history who seemed buried and gone. This is such a time, for me, with the Black Lives Matter movement, for a true reappraisal of slavery in this country and also worldwide. It is all I am thinking about now, because I didn't understand enough of legal matters before, and I want to. The Constitution and capitalism arose together, for instance. The Federal wing of the Government is both intrusive and evasive. Structures we have lived with are not what they seem, or, in fact, *are* what they seem. But we have to have a complete re-education as a nation.

TWR Earlier on, you mentioned women disarming men in relation to vulnerable persons 'at the mercy of the world'. Women have been emancipated somewhat from their subservient position. Now, they may be navigating a world that wasn't set up, as you intimated earlier, either by or for them. What are some of the traits of 'the world' that are in conflict with women's or feminine experience?

FH The adults nearby expect you to turn into 'a sweet person'. Your parents want to protect you from boys and men very early. That boys 'only want one thing' becomes a truism, as they develop with burning desires for instant gratification and goals to grab onto. This sounds very old-fashioned, especially when so much has been accomplished, but these characteristics are hard to erase. Women can be cruel to other women still, competition rules, and they can try to seduce men away from the women they live with. Old stuff. I don't think of even the middle class as being a very protected area for women, or girls, or anyone else who is not a conventional man. It is like a field in which you can be tracked, traced, and targeted. Your generation is now on a very productive hunt for a new class, not middle, but edgy, where the forest meets the field. Whatever it takes, it is a necessary turn.

TWR 'Where the forest meets the field' reminds me of what I see in bewilder: *Be Wilder*. Do you have a sense of when you stopped being a child?
FH I suppose I really stopped when I was between fourteen and seventeen.

TWR Why then?
FH It was a lot to do with household changes: a sister leaving, a sister being born. And I had already decided when I was fourteen that I would be a poet and that I wouldn't let anyone judge me. I think it was a strike for independence, which would be the end of childhood.

TWR What was compelling to you at fourteen about being a poet? Were there specific poets you had in mind?
FH Fortunately, my mother was very Irish and very full of poetry, so it was in the house. There was also my love of the French language: I was reading Baudelaire and Verlaine when I was that age and I was just completely enamoured. I did very badly in school and didn't get accepted to college.

TWR Why do you think you did badly in school?
FH Rebellion, fear of people, and I think my brain is not good at that kind of teaching, where you're asked to go home, remember, and then spit it out. I'll do well at other ways of learning, but not the standard way of the West. I just kept overinterpreting a question and the teachers would get mad at that. If it was geology and they said, 'What does this stone look like to you?' I would start thinking, 'Oh it must have dropped from this place and...'

TWR But you've taught since?
FH I taught for forty-seven years. It was my

penance. I went right to the university. I did some of the Poets in the Schools, which is something good and fun we did in the Seventies, but basically I began and ended teaching in colleges.

TWR What was Poets in the Schools?
FH It was this great movement that Ron Padgett and Kenneth Koch started that involved poets going into public schools in New York, San Francisco, and Boston, teaching kids how to write poetry. Some of the teachers co-operated, some of them were irritated. With the kids, it was very productive. Poets & Writers: I think it became them.

TWR Was it a volunteer effort?
FH Yes. Maybe we got 50 dollars.

TWR Was teaching at the university how you subsisted?
FH I first wrote pulp novels, and that helped me get through about four years. And then I had to teach, my most dreaded idea. By then, I was twenty-seven, and having three children meant I had to be on their schedule.

TWR How did you start writing pulp fiction?
FH I was in California. I had no money. I was not good at anything. So I wrote a story and it was rejected. It was a typical first novel, humiliating.

TWR What's a typical first novel?
FH I mean, it was very blind. It was pretentious and blind at the same time. About a family like my own but I didn't even know it was my family. An idiot's novel. So then I sent it to an agent in New York who wrote back and said, 'Give this up, write some pulp novels, I can tell you know how to tell a story.' He sent me a mountain of these books that used to be called 'Sweet Nurse' books or something. They weren't dirty but there was always a romance. I got the job to write the 'Sweet Nurse' books when I was West, but the *Vietnam Nurse* one [Avon, 1966, authored under the pseudonym Della Field] I wrote in New York. I had to do quite a bit of research. I would go around New York and meet the WAVES [Women Accepted for Volunteer Emergency Service] and the WACS [Women's Army Corps] and talk to them. I had it all down to the formula by then, they took usually six weeks to write. They paid 500 dollars for one. My rent on the Bowery was 200. Later, I wrote young adult books to pay for me and my kids to go away for

two weeks in the summers. By then I was living in Boston and working there.

TWR Were there any writers you tried to emulate?

FH Back in the old days? There were people like Djuna Barnes, Marguerite Duras and Virginia Woolf, *The Golden Notebook*, *Hopscotch*, Latin Americans, Italians, Russians.

TWR Did you write erotic novels too?

FH No. Never.

TWR What about *Forty Whacks*? I'd shelved that 1969 collection in my mind under 'erotica'.

FH *Forty Whacks* was my first collection – it was one long story and five short stories that were an apprenticeship for me. That came out of Houghton Mifflin. It had the suffering sexuality of that age. But it wasn't porn. I really worked on the prose. I got deep into making sentences and sound for the first time. Otherwise, before, I had just spun a good story. The writing of pulp fiction gave me a great respect for storytelling. It's something that I taught myself. I realised there is a kind of ideal: the useless hopeless child goes out in the world, is terrified of leaving, but goes out anyway, and bad things and good things happen. Sort of the idea is you can't go home until you've been completely eviscerated by the outside world.

TWR You describe this archetypal story format in *Night Philosophy*. It reminded me of Joseph Campbell's 'Hero's Journey' [from *The Hero with a Thousand Faces*, 1949], based on studies of the stories of Buddha, Jesus and James Joyce, and Carl Jung's archetypes. This idea that the same story structure or 'monomyth' repeats across time: a journey from the known to the unknown and back.

FH It's just like that. In my nurse books, I had to invent a format for women.

TWR Right, because the popular rehearsals of this story, from Buddha to *Star Wars*, are male-centric. Do you find that the Hero's Journey is true to life?

FH Human development in retrospect, and as I watch my young friends and my kids grow up, does weirdly resemble the classic Hero's Journey – for a while and for people of all ages, genders, and traditions. My nurses had to be good at their jobs and want a man but not sleep with one. They were heroic in that they didn't fall apart. I learned a lot from writing those books, about plot and consequence. We always think we're inventing a new narrative. Now, there are new ways of thinking about the narrative, thanks to female and non-American writers.

TWR Do you think people go through many of these journeys in a lifetime?

FH I do sort of see the spiral that we have maybe four or five such wanderings in our life and that's what makes it confusing. Maybe we should call them Bardos.

TWR Were there phases of your life when you didn't write?

FH I was always writing and moving. They go together for me. Unknown places are fuel for thought.

TWR What life phases – or places – have inspired the most writing?

FH Much as I was homesick in San Diego, that's where I wrote the most. Basically all the novels in *Radical Love* I wrote in San Diego. The one called *Nod*, that was written in Ireland.

TWR Why did San Diego produce so much writing?

FH I was resentful at having to be there, so far from my family, thanks to having no money, that I went into a reclusion state. I would go into my office at seven in the morning and not come out until six. I would keep the office door shut all day.

TWR Does the place you're writing from inform the writing?

FH Yes completely, like being dropped in water. It is the environment.

TWR I'd like to hear more about New York in the Sixties. How long did you live on the Bowery?

FH Not too long, because I got too upset by New York. I would say it was two and a half years.

TWR What upset you?

FH I guess just the old horror of seeing poverty and wealth mashing up. I was used to a different landscape, coming out of Boston. It's a gentler but much more segregated city. Boston is a shadow, you can hide in it. I wasn't used to the rough *laissez-faire* of New York, people lying on the streets, and going mad, and no one caring, everyone walking on. I somehow couldn't stand it. I'm talking about serious Bowery days, Andy Warhol days. I understand why Edie Sedgwick had to leave. She was so vulnerable and nervous, and she grew up on a ranch in Southern California, so she would've been very susceptible.

TWR The poor little rich girl trope. Somehow I associate Edie Sedgwick and Kathy Acker. Maybe it's just the bleached hair, but there's also familial wealth, daddy issues, New York, counterculture, fashion icons.... Has anyone ever tried to make a movie from your books?
FH A couple of people did try. With *Saving History*. Nothing happened.

TWR That's the one I was thinking of. That [1993] novel is so cinematic, and heartbreakingly current. The California/Mexico border setting. A single mother with two children, one sick, in need of an organ transplant; but this justified mistrust of the American health finance system. Motels, cars, an activist lawyer, outlaws, political debate, prison. What kind of research did you do for that novel?
FH It was triggered by a newspaper article by Alexander Cockburn, a British guy who was very Leftist. He was in Mexico and he found out about this horrible trail of children's kidneys. I wrote to him and I did more picking around.

TWR You don't use those terms, but in *Saving History*, it was helpful to me to have a mother/lover's perspective on her attachments to a violent man. 'I live out his drama,' you wrote, 'mentally, trying to imagine the way it felt to be him. I hope that in this imaginative action, some of his pain will revert to me. If I don't do this, who else will? It was her assignment for a few years to receive his blows and his cruel words...'. She flees, but only after many cycles of violence, repentance, sadness, forgiveness. What is this attachment to another's woundedness? Propelling this cycle?
FH I think it's really beyond the individual. It's some kind of capacity that somebody has for reasons we'll probably never understand – a capacity for pity. I think William Blake's whole conception of the word 'pity' is more political than the word 'compassion'. Compassion to me is nonpolitical. But pity is much more tangled and engaged in the problem itself. You pity a person who loses control. Some lawyers I've heard say they feel as sorry for the abuser as they do for the victim, because it's all such a mess, and not something anyone wanted, it's that kind of complicated identification.

TWR There's a quote from you about Simone Weil that reminds me of this. You write: 'Weil felt that one must continually compensate for violence done to others.'
FH Yes. That's very much her thinking.

TWR I first encountered *Saving History* in *Radical Love*, your five-novel collection that I read as one big – spiral, perhaps, like you mention earlier, 'four or five such wanderings in our life...'. Later, to parse each story individually, and because my copy of *Radical Love* was falling apart, I ordered the original editions of each novel, or those I could track down. A few of them were published by Sun & Moon Press. What was that?
FH A wonderful press. Douglas Messerli was the editor. He began with a journal called *Sun & Moon* and then he got more and more focused on a certain kind of experimental, metafiction writer. He sort of saved a generation and he destroyed them too because often he couldn't pull it off. People waited six years for their book to come out, that kind of thing. He meant so well and he was so kind, it was hard to scream at him.

TWR I know the type. Were you working with an agent at the time?
FH Never. I decided that I had no interest in making any money from my writing and I didn't want anyone telling me what to do. That's going back to being fourteen. I had one editor at Houghton Mifflin who was quite interventionist but he was so good at it, I accepted it from him. Chris Kraus [at Semiotext(e)] is a great meticulous editor and so is Kazim Ali [co-founder of Nightboat Press]. Camilla Wells at Divided Press in London is young and alert to error. She was great for *Night Philosophy*.

TWR I keep thinking of that stock interview question about ideal dinner party guests. What about Chris Kraus, Eileen Myles and Ariana Reines? I've seen you read and publish together. That's a dinner party of sorts.
FH It is. What a party. It was so unexpected. Eileen and I have known each other since the Sixties from New York but she's very sort of like a lighthouse, she comes around and disappears and comes back in a pool of light.

TWR Staying with hypothetical dinner parties, your non-fiction-leaning work, from *The Wedding Dress: Meditations on Word and Life* to *Night Philosophy*, directly converses with many writers and historical figures, among them Francis of Assisi, Simone Weil, Michel de Certeau and Thomas Aquinas.

FH [Laughs] I think in that essay I wrote, 'Bewilderment' [collected in *The Wedding Dress*], I have the form or vision of a spiral, where you can't tell if it's going up or down and you keep passing the same people, you even pass yourself going up or going down. And I keep passing those same people over and over again as if I'm caught in a tidepool and I can't resist. I can't not go back to Simone Weil. It's literally like a biological feature of my brain that just goes round and around.

TWR Do you have any way of making sense of that – why these figures?

FH I think it's almost molecular. We all have a fate. Even if that word isn't common now, we know what it means. And your biological fate sort of determines how you react to your original interests. And it somehow never gets solved during your lifetime but you're always trying to solve it. So those figures represent the people who did in a sense solve it for me.

TWR They helped answer some of the big questions?

FH Yeah, and lived it out.

TWR Right. That is a big part of these figures, and how you write about them – they practised their beliefs to extremes. Simone Weil didn't just write about God, war and workers' rights, she went to the factories, to the front lines, had mystical revelations, and might have died on a political hunger strike – although biographers debate this. Do you feel like you've practised your beliefs?

FH Not to the point I wish I had. If I had, I would be dead probably. Or have gone to jail. One or the other.

TWR Yes, what is it... Courage or foolishness, the conviction to *really* live it out...

FH I know. It's interesting for me to see how people are not just remembered for the poem they wrote in 1890, but for the life they led. That still does trail the artist. It's interesting to sort of just wake up to that, because I used to think, 'Oh, if

only I could just write one perfect poem, my life would be justified.' In a way I still do... But, you know what I mean.

TWR If you could ask Simone Weil one question, what would you ask?

FH I would ask her when she was happy. I asked a man I knew once who was a painter, an Italian, *does he remember a time when he was happy*, and he said right away, 'It lasted for three minutes, I was on a train with my mother.' It was beautiful, it was instant.

TWR Is that a question you ask yourself?

FH I do.

TWR And the answer – when are you happy?

FH The safety of an ended day, with children around, beds open, a friend whirling ice around in her glass, music on the box, puzzlement.

TWR It seems to me that you have led a storied life, one that will trail your art. You've engaged in many kinds of activism – what actions have you found to be most effective?

FH I haven't been as great an activist as I would have liked, in terms of belonging to an organisation or organising sit-ins. I admired my friends who did it so much. Teaching is a kind of spoken activism. Neighbourhood work when I was a young mother was the most effective. All else, protests.

TWR What does neighbourhood work mean?

FH We opened a health clinic. It was family health, accessibly priced but anyone who walked in would get care. The doctors worked for Mass General or another hospital, and the hospitals co-operated with these clinics around Boston and gave them like four doctors each. We were going to all the meetings, interviewing doctors, overseeing the establishment of the first one. It was the Seventies, you can imagine people were doing all kinds of neighbourhood fix-ups and housing things. Boston was crackling with ideas for social reforms. These involved knowing where you lived, knowing some neighbours and who the mayor and school committee were, understanding how tenants were living under landlords, and talking on corners with residents. It was practical. Local. I always lived with other people. We all helped with food and children. We started a daycare in the basement and the family clinic down the street. There was violence against women, so there were marches, co-ops behind chicken wire, racist rants, meetings in parks. Much of the political engagement was a reaction to a threat rather than ideological. Poverty was an obstacle, not a condition. We went by car or bus to marches in other cities and of course mobilised them at home. Vietnam, James Brown. Now it's still a question of mobilisation and of figuring out ways to live at the poverty level, with the help of friends. I still stand by people sharing their living, putting children first, their schooling and their outdoor lives. And I miss freedom songs at marches.

TWR I wanted to talk about your family – you come from an expansive artistic and intellectual family. In what ways is your work in conversation with them?
FH I do think that from the moment you're born, you're trying to fuse or choose your parents. Whether they live happily or not, they're always two separate beings; you're always identifying with one or the other and getting confused by that. I had two extremely different parents, one being a civil rights activist and lawyer and the other being an Irish woman passionately in love with the theatre, so it was always a conflict in all of us.

TWR That's one of the defining aspects of your work, and what compels me the most about it: this integration of a civil rights and political conscious-ness with that of a poet and a believer.
FH That is what I was given. I've noticed that the friends of mine who are somewhat poetic and great storytellers often grew up in a family of socialists. It's surprising how much people are trained from an early age to think that way, to talk about it at the table, to watch the news. I was, certainly, although that may not be true of your generation.

TWR I'd like to reiterate how important it has been for me and many of my peers to read your holistic and ambitious yet grounded approach to political and class consciousness, including race and gender intersections *alongside* religious and poetic questioning, beauty, mysticism, myth, emotional psychology, and the everyday texture of it all. There's a tendency to parcel this stuff apart, but it seems necessary to address it all.
FH For reasons I don't have, I was always obsessed with God and meaning, from a very young age, outside of family patterns. Poetry was of course

part of the same kind of thinking, but what I wanted most to read was theology, philosophy and politics. Frantz Fanon, Simone Weil of course, and for years now, Giorgio Agamben and Hannah Arendt, but the great time was when Liberation Theology brought them together. [Roman Catholic priest, theologian, philosopher and social critic] Ivan Illich and Gustavo Gutiérrez [Peruvian philosopher, theologian and Dominican priest regarded as one of the founders of Liberation Theology] developed what for me was the most profound analysis of human nature and political theory. The gospels were the starting point. These were Marxist thinkers who coincided with freedom movements in Africa and Latin America. Liberation Theology spread to many other countries where there was extreme and widespread poverty and made no distinctions between men and women in their possession of dignity. It's all the poor, all the oppressed. The power system that gets into human nature so easily is a problem for everyone. Liberation Theology goes into very profound analysis of how that happens. Radical reforms in rural life – I could go on. But the main thing for me was its foundation in Franciscan theology regarding nature and human nature. This was all a solitary pursuit until I met certain men and women, who in general were Catholic. I've been writing a play about St Francis for ages.

TWR I found a reference in one of your poems, again from *O'Clock*, to Camilo Torres, who is said to be a predecessor of Liberation Theology: 'I still can't kil / my hopes before the strangeness of change / and so I've come to stay / where Camilo Torres says: / "Every Catholic who is not a revolutionary / is living in a state of mortal sin."' Could you tell us more about the St Francis play?
FH Oh, it's so depressing, it really just dissolved after three years of work because of the virus and because Martha Clarke, the choreographer and director, couldn't raise the money in the third year to go forward. It wasn't her fault, everything was about to fall through in the world, I could see it wasn't going to go far. But I believe it will ultimately. Martha is a genius, she's brilliant. I still believe this play will be seen.

TWR At one point in *The Needle's Eye*, you describe St Francis as being a sexy teenager.
FH He was famously lecherous, good-looking,

everybody loved him, and he was a big party guy. And then came a war, and he was very vain, and thought he could be a great soldier, and he was thrown in prison, and that's where he went through his change. Prison is always a motif for me, imprisonment as the most awful thing on earth.

TWR Prison repeats, as do mental institutions. In both *Nod* and *Bronte Wilde*, young rebellious women end up there. In *Nod*, the male doctor's authority (his 'sanity') comes across as pathological, in that it is dependent on the policing of (and fascination with) female 'insanity' – her deviance within his system of meaning. She is able to escape the patriarchal institution when, after repeating 'her story' to him, he falls asleep: 'the Doctor snored. And that was the moment I tiptoed (sick of fiction) past him out of the brick building and set off to exercise my happiness in foreign lands.' I love this implication that the personal narratives we are encouraged to relate under psychiatric care are fictional. Also, the fairy-tale-like language you summon at the end. I'm curious how you've seen mental illness treatment change throughout your lifetime, and if you ever make use of diagnostic terms.

FH I only do if I have to. Like if it's a friend's child, say, and that's the way they talk about it. I am wary of pathology-language, how cruel the words are. You see it especially with children being stigmatised so young, told they're failures in grade three. *Nod* was inspired by reading a dialogue between an Indian therapist and a British one and how they spoke of bodily motions and speech, the massive difference in interpretation. I was fascinated by how one society judges action completely differently to another, and what it would be like to straddle those two, as the girl in *Nod* is trying to do. This word 'narcissism' is so overgeneralised – if someone is conceited for one minute, they're a narcissist. It's self-critical, overly picking the body of the proletariat to bits.

TWR 'The present tense is the tense of emergency and ego,' you write in *Night Philosophy*. 'I don't like it telling a story. The past is the most convincing and carries a shadow on its back like a bag of stones. The past is always a little melancholy. Slate gray, sunless. The past is the best tense for storytelling. The storyteller drops the bag and sits down to look it over.' Do you like the present tense in writing that isn't storied; in poetry or in political manifesto, for instance?

FH I could see that a manifesto would want to be in the present tense. And often a reverie. I think in my book *The Deep North* (Sun & Moon Press, 1988) there were reverie sections which accompany the story. But about twenty years ago, everybody began writing in the present tense, and it was like almost a secret revolution. It was associated with confession, autofiction and all of that, but there's something more to it socially, I think, in a larger way. It's something important about time, and responsibility for it. In any case, it's always best to start fiction with personal experience, even science fiction.

TWR I think that's a very interesting connection – that there has been this rise in immediate-tense autofiction, it's often self-reflexive but in the moment.

FH So there is really a lack of cause and effect. And that's the model of tragedy – cause and effect.

TWR What are you working on now?

FH I don't write fiction any more at all. And poetry demands more scholarship than it used to. Now, at this moment, after doing *Night Philosophy*, I am obsessively thinking about this term *recapitulation* and how it's been used in different disciplines. The 'implicate order' is a term in physics, invented by the great David Bohm, and even ruminations on potentiality carry a similar structure, secret but beautiful. These are all related.

TWR Recapitulation – it sounds almost bureaucratic.

FH It does. Very. The theology is basically that God tried out human nature and it failed right from the get-go, with Adam. And then there were thousands of years of more mistakes being made since the first one. So the recapitulation is a backward look at where we/you have come from in order to assess the damage and try again. The hidden subject is failure.

F. A. D.,
August 2020

JACK UNDERWOOD

POETRY

POEM BEGINNING WITH A LINE FROM ANNA SEWARD

But oh with pale, and warring fires, decline
the waking tasks, if that's what you need.
You don't have to compete with business.
You don't have to compete with me, moving things
from room to room, nurturing distraction.
Shut the hillside behind you. Burn whatever forest.
I can water the smouldering animals.
If you need me to tie your hair back, I will learn
to tie your hair back well. If you need me to pass
this week over to the saints, I will guide them
through orientation. If you are unsure
what you want from life, and include me
in that confusion, I can still offer water,
or else go back downstairs to sit and stir,
on your behalf, this brilliant white emulsion.

THE LANDING
for Nancy Agnes

You come/ round thinking
in a new language/of the familiar
your voice/ dragging at my body
my body/ still waking
but already/ I'm on the landing
I'm reaching you/ awake now
my hand/ in the black
finding the back /of your sweaty
little head/ *I'm here I'm here...*
to settle /you again
into sleep/ and inside
your neat organs/are working
your lungs/ I can hear
are filling/ with the air
the food/ in your stomach
I cooked for you/ today
the piss/ in your bladder
and the shit/ in your colon
the bile/ your pancreas
your liver/ like the offal
of a song bird/ neat and dark
and busy/ and your feet
like rare cave mushrooms
your eyelashes/ and hair
which you've grown/ from nothing
made/ for yourself
for your life/ by your mother
from nothing/ and I'm filled
I'm filled/ with the fear
of the joy/ no the sadness
of the joy/ a leaf
on a street/ what I mean
if you don't know/ what I mean
by the sadness/of the joy
is forgive me/ I mean don't worry
about it/ for a second
if you don't/ but if you do
know what I mean/ and I'm still
alive to tell/please
please come/ and tell me
about it/ I'm here
I'm here/ I'll never leave this room.

BLOOD CLOT IN A WINTER LANDSCAPE

I have become closer to the rock,
much to the jealousy of the shadow
of the rock and the sunlight that falls
upon the rock, though none compete
with the damp earth beneath the rock,
the mutual weight of that affection.
But what of the coin put there, on top,
meaning to mean, but what? That a mind
has actioned here? That a motionless love
might be expressed through deliberate
non-verbal gestures? Can we make love,
not in the midst of a winter landscape,
but with the winter landscape itself?
Can I fall afterwards exhausted upon it,
the snow falling exhausted upon me?
Or else be wakened by a clot of blood
in the middle of that winter landscape,
a clot that ushers me to my feet saying
come on – there are portals – opening
in your mouth – right now – every word –
another dimension – these are graveside
aggregates – a ladle decanting – punchbowl
to punchbowl – honest as rock – I promise
– you're not dreaming – of somewhere else –
in your body – that both of us should be –

ERRATA

My grandfather, dying, explained
that *letting go* is the easy part;
you can only do half the job,
the rest, he said, is up to God,
or time, which is the same thing,
though I'm sure I've not remembered
or measured it correctly, maybe
someone else's grandfather or
crossing a border on horseback or
was it, then, a butterfly already on
the wing, the fog was rising – *I must
go in* – but in this version a boat
is getting quietly away at night,
a rope hauled through dark water
by a hand that reaches to find
the edge of a table, and retreats,
nothing permanent upturned.

ADAM PENDLETON

'How do you respond to state-sanctioned physical and intellectual brutality? How do you respond collectively?' US-born artist Adam Pendleton's answer takes its cue from the post-First World War Dada movement, which rejected the bourgeois aesthetics that governed capitalist society and sought to disrupt its structures of logic and reason, and from LeRoi Jones's 1964 poem 'Black Dada Nihilismus'. His *Black Dada Reader* (2017) – initially produced as a spiral-bound pamphlet for distribution among friends; later an acclaimed artist's book – contains photocopied texts by artists, writers and activists including Stokely Carmichael, Harryette Mullen, Gertrude Stein, Sun Ra, Adrian Piper, Ad Reinhardt, Hugo Ball, Stan Douglas, June Jordan, Félix González-Torres and W. E. B. Du Bois. Forming a personal sourcebook of the twentieth-century avant-garde, which stages and challenges the interlocking relationships between language, civil rights, conceptual art and history, the book – and connected artworks – offers 'a way to talk about the future while talking about the past'.

Pendleton's work brings together a multiplicity of sources and ideas in 'radical juxtapositions to disrupt established history and open up new potential associations'. His 2005 show *Deeper Down There* showcased screenprints featuring lines from African-American poets and songwriters including Toni Morrison and Audre Lorde; his 2016 show *Becoming Imperceptible* took its title from the writings of Gilles Deleuze and Félix Guattari and drew on political and artistic movements from Conceptualism and Minimalism to Black Resistance, incorporating found images and footage from civil rights protests, Jean-Luc Godard films, African art and Bauhaus experimentation. The monochromatic works shown here take fragments of Sol LeWitt's *Incomplete Open Cubes* (1974), cropped or enlarged from photocopies using a scanner, and overlaid by single or multiple letters from the phrase 'Black Dada', set in Arial Bold. Language and form are abstracted, removed from their original context and collaged into new associations, definitions and meanings. His series *Untitled (WE ARE NOT)* (2019–), a selection from which is shown here, alludes to Tristan Tzara's 'Manifesto of Monsieur Antipyrine', delivered in 1916 at the first Dada soirée in Zurich ('We are not naive / We are successive / We are exclusive'). Precise and minimalist, yet containing multitudes of ideas, stories and events within them, Pendleton's works create the material conditions and conceptual framework for new forms of expression and self-definition.

PLATES

XXV	*Untitled (A Victim of American Democracy)*, 2016	
XXVI	*Untitled (A Victim of American Democracy)*, 2017	
XXVII	*Untitled (WE ARE NOT)*, 2019	
XXVIII	*Untitled (WE ARE NOT)*, 2019	
XXIX	*Untitled (Who We Are)*, 2019	
XXX	*Untitled (WE ARE NOT)*, 2020	
XXXI	*Black Dada (A/A)*, 2019	
XXXII	*Black Dada Drawing (A)*, 2018	
XXXIII	*Black Dada Drawing (B)*, 2018–19	
XXXIV	*Black Dada Drawing (C)*, 2018–19	
XXXV	*Black Dada Drawing (D/D)*, 2018	

I

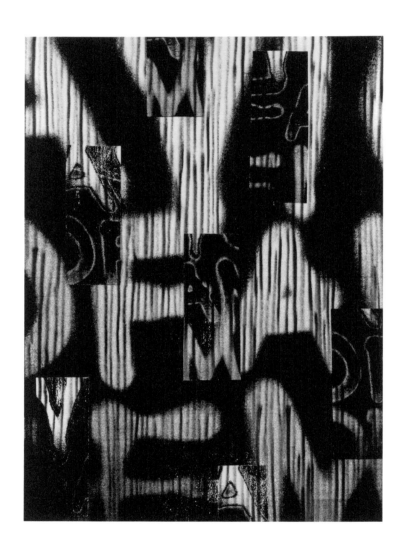

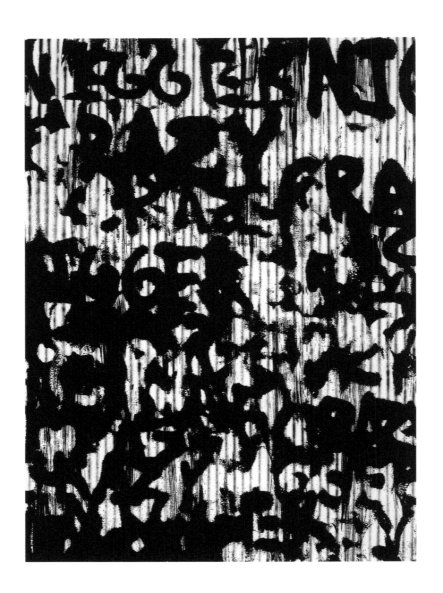

XXIX

II

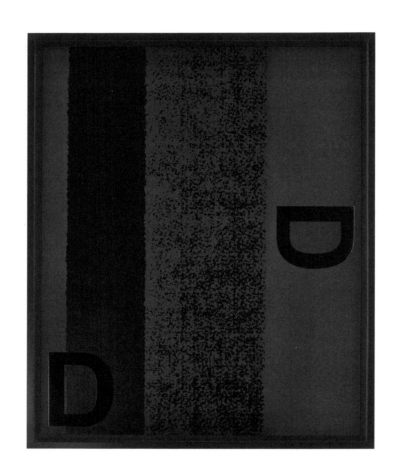

TWO STORIES

ILYA LEUTIN
tr. ANNA ASLANYAN

DICTATORS' HANDS

There are different versions as to what happened to the hands of the Argentine dictator Juan Perón, allegedly stolen after his death; namely:

— only the hands were stolen;
— the hands and forearms were stolen;
— the entire arms were stolen;
— it was Eva Perón's hands rather than Juan's that were stolen;
— both Juan's and Eva's hands were stolen;
— no hands were stolen whatsoever.

These allegations gave rise to a spate of myths in Argentina, their particulars dependent on a given administrative division. The residents of Buenos Aires believe it all to be lies: the dictator's extremities were never stolen, and even if they were, it was most likely only the hands, nothing more. The further away from the capital city, the more radical the local take on the story. People living as far as Ushuaia, for instance, are convinced that the entire arms were cut off, all the way up to the shoulders.

If you happen to find yourself in the highest circles of Latin American society, you'll notice that there the story accumulates certain further details:

— the first, possibly the only, collector of leaders' and dictators' hands was Pablo Escobar, the famous Colombian drug lord;
— the hands are collected by a member of a well-known family, which owns several factories, one of them being a manufacturer of clothing zips, a subsidiary of the Japanese industry giant YKK;
— the hands are collected by a member of the world shadow government;
— no one collects anyone's hands – it's all rumours.

In addition to Juan Perón's hands, those of Jorge Videla and the Chilean general Augusto Pinochet are also mentioned. Some people, fairly significant figures in Argentina's political and social life, believe that:

— Juan Perón's hands are kept in a private collection in Colombia;
— Augusto Pinochet's hands are exhibited in an unknown collector's home gallery in London;
— the embalmed hands of a number of dictators are stored in the same place, in Argentina, and some informants have even seen the collection with their own eyes.

Let me remind you that these are all mere speculations and rumours, and as such should not necessarily be taken for granted. If you stay in Latin America for a little longer than a holiday, such deviant factoids and sometimes also real facts – the discrepancy between the two being admittedly negligible there, much more so than anywhere else – cease to surprise you. I would never write any of this were it not for an acquaintance of mine, N, who once, over dinner, told me something else. I take his words seriously and can vouch that N wasn't lying or mocking me. If what he told me bears little resemblance to the truth, one can only conclude that he, too, is in thrall to the myth prevalent in Latin America.

Allow me to refrain from naming him. I have enjoyed a friendly relationship with this prominent Argentine industrialist of Italian descent over the past two years. I am a decent golf player, and it was this sport that engendered our fellow feeling, which has subsequently grown, I'll venture to say, into a reserved friendship. Having used the word, I am not entirely sure if people of his status can even have friends. I am conscious of the fact that one could, if one wanted to, easily guess who he is. He found the whole story quite mundane and amusing. He is slightly over sixty, keeps himself in a good shape, likes a spot of sailing, a spot of baccarat, poker and golf, all that without ever losing his head. He sees golf as some kind of compromise between sport and entertainment. Our acquaintance implied no commitment, I was friendly with him without trying to ingratiate myself, and that must have won him over. That and, needless to say, my skills when it came to choosing a club and hitting a hole in one. We used to meet on the course once a fortnight or so until I moved to Los Angeles for a long period of time. One day I received a letter from him, in which he said that he was planning to attend some forum and could try to find the time to see me should I be up for it. I was, of course, in favour and suggested that we play, as in the good old days, but he excused himself, mentioning ankle pain. We went to watch a New York vs Lakers game, cheered the players and then had dinner together. It was the season dubbed the Arab Spring, and TV screens were noisily trumpeting the last throes of the regimes in Egypt, Syria and Libya. Over dinner N said: 'I think Gaddafi will soon say goodbye to his hands.'

I assumed it to be an idiomatic expression I'd never heard and asked him to elaborate. N enquired if I knew about Perón's, Videla's and Pinochet's missing hands.

I was, of course, familiar with the apocryphal story.

N said that if it was indeed apocryphal, it still shaped reality to a greater extent than many actual events did.

'You know who really believes in all these yarns? The rulers. They are the only hostages of this factoid.'

I asked him to explain, and N told me this.

'Every American dictator is afraid of having his hands cut off after his death. He can't ignore this thought because everything works differently in the highest circles. On that level, nothing is impossible. A certain very influential person is interested in expanding his collection. Influential, you see. Do you know what that means? Do you think there was no guard at Pinochet's funeral a year ago? Of course there was. Yet he was still buried without his hands.'

I enquired how N knew that. The information, he said, had been imparted by his father. Of course I chose not to show that I had my reservations about such a source.

N went on to tell me more.

'I once talked to Chávez, quite informally, at a large economic forum. It was he who told me about Videla's hands. He wasn't joking, and you know what? He laughed at the Castro clan because Fidel had got Raúl to promise, in writing, to cremate his body within two hours of his death. His own brother, in writing – can you imagine? Castro himself is afraid of these vandals. But it's no use, Chávez said, because in Latin America, where national currencies are devoured by fierce inflation, the only price that remains constant is the price of dictators' hands.'

After our meeting I grew curious and went online to see who N's father was. I found N's biography, which said that his father had been an Italian immigrant, a small business owner, and that after taking over his father's company, N had brought it to a national level. It seemed unlikely that this man could have had access to any secret documents or highly placed individuals. Then I realised that far from referring to his biological father, N meant the person who had granted him life in big business.

Then I came across a video of Pinochet's funeral, which you can also watch online. It happened in 2010: hundreds of Chileans protested; there were shouts about this murderer finally dying, having long retired from affairs to live the rest of his life peacefully, visiting friends, remaining immune from any prosecution. In the video Pinochet lay among flowers in his coffin, its lower part closed. The general was peeping out from the upper part as if from a nest box, and you could not make out the lower half of his body. Nor his hands, needless to say. Who knows, perhaps those hands were the price he had to pay for his peaceful later years and natural death.

The whole story occurs to me in the following light. The main thing here is a psychological detail that constitutes an additional piece of information contributing to our understanding of the image of dictators in Latin America and perhaps elsewhere. No one is insured against human deviance. For every maniac there is another, even more insane pervert somewhere. Suppose it's true that Chávez, Castro and whoever else might be involved are living in fear of being dishonoured after their death. That creates a field of charming vulnerability around them. At this point we shall leave them alone with themselves, their monarchial solitude and their own hands.

CHICKENS, THEIR NECKS WRUNG

Late in the evening, someone rapped on the window: it sounded like war. Mum pulled back the curtain and her face fell; Dandelion climbed out of the armchair. While she was looking for her housecoat, he was jumping up and down with curiosity. Bowing to the low lintel, two huge men appeared on the threshold: one thin, with a multicoloured hat perched on his head; the other with a moustache, as wheat-blond as Dandelion's hair. Their arrival caused such a hullaballoo in the house, it felt like all the windows and doors had been thrown open. The one with the moustache started tossing Dandelion up in the air, saying in a booming voice, Daddy's back, remember Daddy, eh, and then he tickled Dandelion's stomach, which didn't feel tickly, though it was funny all the same. Dandelion couldn't remember the man at all. His rough skin smelled of tobacco, of yellowness and moustache, and each time he pulled a funny face it made Dandelion fall about with laughter, while Mum stood by the door jamb, dour and kind of detached. The boy forgot about her for a few minutes, and then he felt ashamed of it. Dad rambled, pointing at the one with the hat: 'This is Seny, mate, he's a real captain. He'll tell you all about his adventures if you ask him.' The man proffered Dandelion his long, splayed fingers to shake.

There were buttons of various colours and sizes sewn onto the hat; as for Senymate himself, he was unshaven, spindly and giraffe-like, not looking much like a captain, more like a tramp, but still Dandelion stared at him in admiration.

'You like my hat?'

Dandelion nodded.

'A trophy.'

'He has walked all over Crimea in it. C'mon, Seny, mate, don't be a tight-arse, let the lad have a go.'

'Here you are.' Senymate threw the button hat onto the boy's head. 'Make sure you give it back, though. It's a memento.'

Dandelion didn't know yet what Crimea was. A cone-shaped, hood-like word, sharp at the top and curving towards the bottom, it was easy to put on your head, just like this: crimea. The hat was too big, but his ears kept it in place.

'Why are you here?' Mum suddenly asked, her voice a bit hoarse, her face gone instantly pale.

'To be with you two.'

'You think you're welcome here?'

Dad gave a little whistle.

'Well I never...' He turned to Dandelion. 'Hear that, mate?' Dad smiled, getting the boy on his side. Mum looked angry, Dad took her by the elbow and dragged her out to the porch, shutting the door, leaving Dandelion in the entrance hall with Senymate. They remained silent for a few moments.

'Go on then, show us your room.'

Being in the room with Senymate was boring. He tried to make Dandelion laugh, telling him pirate stories, but he sounded like a liar. He probably wasn't a real captain.

When Mum came back, quite calm now, Dad said he was going to fire up the bathhouse. 'And tomorrow,' he told Dandelion, 'we're going to look for work, me and Seny, mate, at a real poultry farm. Because we've gotta help you, haven't we? When you grow up you'll be helping your own too.'

Mum didn't let Dandelion go to the bathhouse because he had recently had a fever. Dad kept saying that a steam bath would cure anything, so they nearly had another row over it, but after a long argument Dad gave up, and Dandelion stayed in the house. Afterwards, when Dad and Senymate, wrapped in towels and bathrobes, drank their tea, steam was coming off their shoulders and heads, an almost invisible steam, the same as was coming off the saucers they were drinking from.

At night Mum and Dad slept in the same bed, and Dandelion heard them whispering in the room, talking to each other, even arguing, it seemed. They made a bed for Senymate in Dandelion's room, on the floor, and he snored all through the night like a man possessed and wouldn't let Dandelion sleep.

In the morning Senymate got up before everyone else, made some rustling noises in the kitchen and went out for a smoke a few times. Then he sat in the armchair, idly leafing through Mum's letters that were stacked in the cupboard, behind the glass. Dad woke up by lunchtime, stretched, ate in silence, took the letters from Senymate and said it was time they got going. There were blue tattoos on his chest and arm, right below the shoulder: some words and patterns, faded, scribbled, unidentifiable.

Dad and Senymate were out all day, and they didn't come back in the evening either. Dandelion went around the house wearing the button hat, and Mum kept asking him to take it off because it was so dirty: look, the brims are all greasy like pig fat. But Dandelion wouldn't take it off, he could see ripe wheat fields the colour of Dad's moustache, and neither those fields nor Dad's moustache had absolutely anything to do with the rubbery, unpleasant-tasting pig fat he and Mum sometimes had.

Mum made him read a few pages from *The Three Musketeers* before bed, and then it was bedtime, and they turned in without Dad. In the early hours there was a knock on the door, and Mum opened it. Dandelion woke up too and ran out into the hall in his pyjamas. Dad and Senymate each had a sack in their hands. The sacks filled the hall with a smell like you get from big dogs' mouths. Both men were agitated; they were packing their things in a great hurry. Dad put his hand on Dandelion's head.

'Daddy's leaving,' he said, 'you'll be the man of the house now. Get it?' He kissed Dandelion on the head, turned him around with a single movement of his hand and lightly slapped his cold bum. 'Off to bed now, quick.'

Dandelion ran back to his room. Senymate called after him:

'Hey, I need my hat back.'

'You meanie, can't you just let the lad have it?'

'But it's a trophy.'

'Well, you'll fight again to get another.'

They left one sack in the hall; Senymate slung the other over his shoulder and took it with him. For a few more minutes you could hear noises in the hall: Mum's whisper bursting into cries. Then the door slammed hard, and Mum stood in the hall and wept for a long time to the sound of water splashing into the steel sink. Dandelion lay in bed, listening and looking at the ceiling, at a strip of light from the lantern outside. He'd never see Dad again. The sack left propped against the wall was stuffed to the brim with chickens, their necks wrung.

ON WATER
VICTORIA ADUKWEI BULLEY

& we say to her
what have you done with our kin that you swallowed?
& she says
that was ages ago, you've drunk them by now.
– Danez Smith, 'dream where every black person is standing by the ocean'

The atoms of those people who were thrown overboard are out there in the ocean even today
– Christina Sharpe, *In The Wake: On Blackness and Being*

of / water / rains & / dead
– M. NourbeSe Philip, *Zong! #5*

The beaches of Benin are empty. From Cotonou to Ouidah. I have never seen beaches so empty before. From the windows of our minivan, the coastline is a wide expanse of sand beginning just beyond the road, on and on, and then water. Palm trees here and there, but emptiness, mostly. Nobody, no livestock, just sand. As for us, we are eight women and we have just arrived. Three of us – myself included – flew in from London, with the five others coming in from the States. All of us have flown in from winter. It is January, and on our first full day together, our bare skin re-colouring in the light, we ask the driver to take us to a restaurant for lunch. We are seeking the kind of seafood of which we are all so starved, and when our dishes arrive they don't disappoint. Each platter careens with fried plantain, grilled fish, yam, rice, and prawns so large they're not prawns any more but *gambas*, instead. Gambas or langoustines or crayfish or crawfish, depending on which of us is speaking, or who cares to know the difference. Whatever any of it is called, we resolve that we would like to return to eat it again, here, at this terraced balcony from which we watch the sea. The restaurant sits on a beach that is vacant as far as our sight can reach. There is a mutedness to the expanse of the sand, and though it looks no different now than it would at any other time, the staff tell us that yesterday a boy drowned nearby.

The beaches of Benin are empty. At the table, Laurence, who is Beninoise and has family living in the country, says it is because the people remember the history of what happened here. Berlin-drawn nation states aside, and though London is home as best I know it, I call myself Ghanaian. Relative to Benin, that's westward, two borders away. Aniké, also London-based, is from Nigeria, next door, to the east. It is my first time in Benin, but I've been to Nigeria; albeit too briefly, to Lagos. Between the hotel in Ikoyi and the venue of the poetry festival that my friend Belinda and I took part in, we didn't catch much more than traffic. But on the final day, after events had finished, we took a boat ride to a secluded mainland spot. More on that boat ride, later. The place was somewhat out of the way, but the beach there had people on it, as expected. The coastlines of Ghana are likewise full – of people, and often plastic: the blight and detritus of global commerce. In abundance are bars and tourist spots, tin-roofed shacks, and beaten canoes that stay afloat nonetheless, still bringing a day's catch ashore, *but by His grace* – as is painted in cursive on their sides – or something like it. In Jamestown, Accra, the coast is the dwelling place of the fisherfolk I descend from. From here, in any direction, from Cape Coast to Ada, the beaches are populated. From here, too, along the same stretch of land are serial points of other kinds of departures, and the fortifications, dilapidated or preserved, that mark the scale of them.

What happened in Ghana happened in Benin also. And in Nigeria, and in Senegal, and in Angola, and in Cameroon, and in Ivory Coast, and so on and so forth across the Atlantic, or if unluckier still, down, down, into the ocean's bottomless gut. The trade in human lives is old news across the West African coast. So old, perhaps, that if you didn't know what happened, and if you were not there – which you weren't – and if history spoke less about it than it already does, then you might walk its trails and marketplaces without knowing what occurred. And if it had nothing to do with the tourist economy from which they are driven by poverty to make a living, even locals might not tell you. The present has problems of its own, even if the root is shared. But in Benin, the past is loud. The land remembers and the sea does, too.

*

On a trip to Cornwall with T, water is everywhere. We walk and walk, as we like to do, and everywhere we tread are hills and between them, in the furrows of the West Country's brow, streams and rivers, startling in their clarity. When we first arrive, I state an intention to myself that I would like to see some wells. I've only ever seen one before, and on our first day out walking we happen upon my second without looking. A holy one, at the foot of a hill across an open field, in a village called St Neot – for whom the well is named. It is walled away, behind a door that I want to open. I attempt to get closer, but I am wearing the wrong footwear. The grass in front of it is thick with water and my shoes sink up to their laces.

I don't know what it is that makes a well holy, so I set about discovering. It is likely that there are as many answers to this as there are wells in the world, but here are two most applicable to the West. The typical plot is simple: some holy person called for water to spring forth in a particular place, and so it did. Sometimes the person was holy before it happened, which is why it worked. Other times, it was the birth of the spring that sealed the deal. In other cases, the well is discovered to have healing properties in search of which the beleaguered faithful will travel from near and far.

*

A Guide to Building a Well.

Freshwater. All need it, but not all have it. For reasons mostly not unpolitical. Let's say this time it's you that doesn't have any, and nobody's going to run a television commercial somewhere overseas asking for donations to furnish you with some. No sliding violins for you. If you have the tools – and if there are no leaky pipelines, lead leachings, or agricultural contaminants – you dig a well. Maybe you're at risk already but you dig a well anyway, because needs must and you'll die soon otherwise. Perhaps you find a forked twig of hazel to dowse with, first. There are people who can do that, even now. Either way, you dig. You dig (and *dig*, and *dig*) like your life depends upon it, because it does. It might be hard, but dying may be harder. You continue, you dig and dig (and *dig*, and *dig*) as the ground grows damp, then wet, then sodden, and you keep digging, still, until what you're bailing out is more water than clayed or chalky earth; until there's so much water that you couldn't keep digging even if you wanted to. Then you wait for the water to settle clear. You hope that it does.

*

During a residency on an island off Salvador, Brazil, we are taken to another holy water place. A man had a dream once, goes the story. He was blind, but in a sleep vision he received instructions to be led by the hands of two young virgins into a forest. There, he would come upon a pool of spring water – the location of which the two girls would know – and once there, he was to wash his eyes in it. If he did this, his eyes would see again. He did it, and they did. Now, so moved was he by this that he vowed to live at the site permanently, becoming a healer for any who came to him seeking restoration. He became well-known and sought-after as the hermit of that place, until, in a battle for land – which is always to say, *profit* – he was forcibly removed. He made a second vow, then: this time, not to eat until he could return. He never did make it back but the site, with its pool of water, became a sanctuary.

Our guide, Augusto, tells us this story before we head into the forest. As he speaks, the air is charged with the wing-music of cicadas, a sound I hear now for the first time. We wander in and myriad insects greet us with thirsty enthusiasm. Augusto slaps his calves so impressively hard that the clap of palm against skin echoes far into the trees and disturbs birds. I pause to crouch at intervals and watch a millipede passing; a line of large black ants each diligently carrying a fresh cut of leaf. It moves me no end to observe the graceful collectivity of their work. Augusto calls my name, lest I am left behind. I rise and catch up with the others. It is humid and we are bitten so we are fortunate not to have to walk for long, and we approach the site of the pool without trouble. I ready myself for how the water might feel between my toes or trickling through my scalp. It is good to cool one's head, one's *ori*, regularly.

But when we get there, we find nothing. The pool is dry. I stare at the ground where it should have been, pushing my fingers into its sandy bed.

The water is gone – has been going, we are told – because of excessive cattle farming uphill. In the gamble between a sacred spring and a growing demand for beef, beef had won.

*

I have a practised habit of asking about the past, a trait probably cultivated since I came into speech. I liked to ask *why* a lot. *Why*, perhaps more than *what, where, when,* and even *how,* is always a question about the past. Questions of *what* and *where* risk fooling us into thinking that our answers can be clean and numerical. What happened? *This.* Where? *It was there.* When? *Then.* How? *Like so. Why*, though, is where things get muddy. It is where the human voice enters – and for some, that of God – or failing this, for lack of answers, it is where the arms fall helpless at one's sides. It is at *why* that the past frays and scatters, and I find myself writing to keep what I have of it close and whole. Things fall apart and, long before they do, they yellow at their edges – a gradual disappearance at play even when events are not wilfully forgotten but instead brought purposefully to light.

But that isn't all of it. I know I do not always need to keep the past because I know, too, that it is present in spite of me. It is here whether we like it or not. In bad times, the past is a party. In good times, it's the present that is, and the past is a stranger, gate-crashing.

Your hair is like my grandmother's hair, my mother would say when

I was young. Standing in her room while she folded linen, I would ask about this woman whom she often mentioned. *What was it like?* Long, but kept covered. *When was she born?* I don't know. *When did she die?* The Seventies. *What did she look like?* She was fair-skinned, a mix of something.

And what was her name?

Robesa. Robesa Nelson. *Nelson.*

*

When I was fourteen, I came across Brazilian music. Journalling, late at night, I would listen to a radio show on Smooth called *The Late Lounge*, hosted by Rosie Kendrick. Rosie's voice was honey-glazed – husky, you might say. One evening, Rosie played a song that stayed with me and continues to do so. For no real reason. Just the progression of the melody and the calm in the voice that carries it, half in Portuguese, half in English. *Just like this rainstorm / this August day song / I dream of places far beyond.* I scoured the internet for the show's setlist, then set about illegally downloading the song from Limewire. That was what you had to do back then. When I found it, it was called 'August Day Song', and sung by Bebel Gilberto, a daughter of the famed Brazilian Popular Music dynasty. It was the King Britt remix, and I played it on repeat for days, as if to bring Bebel's voice with me through whatever it was that troubled me at the time. *Ouvindo a chuva cair / No cinza um brilho aqui / Fico sózinha, distraída.* I didn't know what the words meant, but a part of me did, and that part was right. *Listening to the rain fall / in the grey, a brilliance here / I am alone, distracted.* Bebel sings each phrase like it's thick with feeling, like she is wanting somebody to know she is waiting for them. The waiting is long and painful, but it will be worth it. *Não vou chorar / Quando lembrar / Do seu eterno olhar.* It will be worth it, yes. There are types of pain that are sweet. This is usually called longing. The Brazilians and Portuguese call it *saudade*. They also say that this word can never be translated, which means to me that it *is* longing, the realest type, the kind where you've got it bad: longing, and then some. And then, next in the song, a gift in the bridge out of the chorus, gentle as a nudge from the universe. *Mesmo tom / Memo som / Como é bom, tão bom.* The *tão bom* is the point of catharsis in the song: its final two words; its two last notes. *Tão bom.* I sing it to myself the way she does, the way she holds the end note until her voice fades out of the room and she's gone, completely.

'How it's *good*,' she sings, '*so good*.'

*

Since the arrival of European colonists, the indigenous peoples of what is now Brazil have faced decimations akin to those met by the Native and First Nations peoples of North and Central America. Like them, they continue to battle for the right to the richness of their languages, their lands and their lives. Like them, too, their genocide is a saga yet to end, let alone to be acknowledged as such. This is the context in which, in 1998, the then-federal deputy for the Christian Democratic Party, Jair Bolsonaro, told the *Correio Braziliense* newspaper that 'it's a shame that the Brazil cavalry hasn't been as efficient as the Americans, who exterminated the Indians.' Two decades later, in 2017, and on film, Bolsonaro was applauded at a members' club when he boasted that, should he become president, 'there [would be] not a centimetre demarcated for indigenous reservations, or quilombolas'.[1] In 2018, speaking to *Globo News*, he adjusted his words, clarifying that he meant 'not one millimetre'. These sentiments manifest through the actions of the oil, mining and agribusiness industries; research published this year by Brazilian non-governmental organisation SOS Mata Atlântica found a twenty-seven per cent increase in tropical deforestation dating from the start of the new presidency.

In the wake of the machinery of the Portuguese settler colonial project – the last to abolish slavery, in 1888 – and the post-independence Brazilian state that followed, something additional is evident: Brazil feels like a black country. This is to say that in spite of the structural whiteness of the state, the culture that Brazil most parades and conceals – through music, dance and cuisine, for example – is black. Even beyond this, even the cadence of the spoken Portuguese sounds black, to me, as a listener. And how else could it be, when forty per cent of the enslaved taken from the African continent came to Brazil, leaving Brazil with the largest population of black people outside of Africa. Interestingly, to this day, the percentage of people self-identifying as black in Brazil is *also* around forty per cent. Less than half the population – and depending upon where you are in the vastness of the country, that's not impossible. That is, if people are telling the truth.

During my residency in Brazil, for which I am researching some family history, I spend time in both Rio de Janeiro and Salvador de Bahia. In Rio, I have the great fortune of having Rui, who is my guide. We are age-mates and we have the same sense of humour, which gives our itinerary the feel of us just hanging out. He has tanned skin, dark eyes, lips not to be squinted at, and hair that curls. So I ask him if he is, and he says *yes, I am, I'm white*.

I tell him how crazy that sounds to me, picturing him on a street in England, and we both laugh. Here begins a new game, a simple one, which goes like this. I discreetly pick someone – anyone – then turn to him:

What about them?

Who? Which one?

That one. There, I nod. *In the grey dress. What might they be?*

And Rui tells me. End of game. Simple.

Or not. Skin tone is one thing, he explains, but to arrive at a more definitive conclusion you must couple that with the texture of the hair, the shape of the nose, the mouth. There are those who look white – like *white* white – but the hair gives it away. Or would, if it could – if it wasn't straightened. Or it doesn't because regardless of what their great-grandmother may have looked like, it is indeed straight; a curl-less gene in the helical swirl of their deoxyribonucleic acid. A phenotypical roulette.

On one of our trips to visit people who could be helpful to my research, Rui takes me to meet Liv Sovik, a professor at the Federal University of Rio de Janeiro. Liv is an American. Blonde-haired, blue-eyed, *white* white. We have a lively discussion about the construction

---

1 Historic Afro-Brazilian communities originally founded by fugitive Africans escaping enslavement.

of race in Brazil. It is a central focus in her work, and likewise her book, the title of which is *Aqui Ninguem é Branco*.

In English: *Here Nobody Is White*.

*

Tracing one's lineage across the Atlantic from the Americas to Africa depends on a few things that read distressingly trivially on paper but make all the difference to where we can say we come from. I say *we*, here, to mean anybody black with the legacy of the trade in their blood. Ultimately, that's all of us. But this particular *we* refers to those who descend from the people who survived those crossings. I want to say, clearly now, something that is often forgotten: this *we* exists on the African continent, too – not just in the Americas and Caribbean. But more on that later. My point is, the story of lineage is long and contingent. As much depends upon who tricked whom, who was encouraged to war with whom (and who lost), who struck deals for guns, rum and cloth, who was exchanged for said items, who was geographically at an advantage – sometimes in the interior, other times at the coast – as it does upon where the boat stopped off at the other edge of the sea.

*

On a street in Jamestown, Accra, is a yellow building. You'll know it when you see it because unlike a lot of the colonial-era buildings, it looks good today. You'll also know it because, of course, it is bright yellow. The name of the building is Brazil House. The street it is on is called Brazil Lane. It was built by refugees from Brazil who had first stopped off at the coast of Nigeria but for some reason had chosen to continue on to Accra, where they were warmly accepted by the local Ga community. When they arrived from across the sea, they spoke neither Ga nor Ewe, nor Fante, nor any other language that was remotely local. They spoke Portuguese. When they were greeted, they would reply, '*ta bom*, which in today's language is the same as saying *it's all good*. It stuck. They became known as the *Tabom*.

*

What little Portuguese I do know, I know because of music. It was through drums that I understood first. The type you hear when you think of Brazilian *carnaval*. The kind of rich, layered, wall-of-sound percussion you might think of when you hear the word *samba* or, if you are more familiar with the music, *maracatú*. The first time I heard this kind of drumming – the origins of which, through the enslaved, were imported from Africa – something in me said yes, deeply. I haven't had many *deep yes* moments in my life. I have resigned myself to the possibility that I am just not one of those lucky people who always knows what they want, whether to decline or accept, stay or go. *Deep yes*es don't come easily to me, but when they do, I know the past is present.

Another Brazilian song that I came across in my mid-teens is a version of 'Aguas de Março', sung live by Elis Regina in a black-and-white video you can find on YouTube. The song, its cyclical lyrics and the footage are hypnotic. If someone were to play me the song on loop, I am certain that I would still not go mad. The lyrics circle over themselves and, like the Bebel Gilberto song, are dense with meaning even in their simplicity.

'A stick / a stone / it's the end of the road / it's the rest of a stump / it's a little alone' are the opening words, penned by Antônio Carlos Jobim. Long before I travelled to Brazil, before I realised its history had anything significant to do with me, 'Aguas de Março' – which translates as 'The Waters of March' – was my entry point into the Portuguese language. If ever you want to learn some basic vocabulary, this song is a good place to start.

·

Some of the enslaved Africans in Brazil were taken from parts of West Africa where Islam was the presiding religion. Arabic influence has a long colonial history across the African continent, one that exponentially pre-dates the arrival of Europeans. In both cases, enslavement ensued, but beyond that, things played out differently. Within the Islamic African context, eventual manumission was possible through conversion from 'heathenism' into the faith. This, and also that you could not be born a slave. Even if your mother was one, you might simply be born into the ruling culture and taken as its own – albeit at low regard. By and large, in the trade instigated by Europeans, no such thing was possible.

In Brazil, the enslaved who were from Islamic cultures were referred to as *malês*. It is believed that this comes from the Yoruba term *imalé* for Muslim. Perhaps they were Yoruba Muslims. Either way, they were put to work in different ways compared to those who were not Muslims. This was for one simple reason: they could read and write in Arabic, which made them useful for tasks that necessitated accounting, and so while they were not free, they had freedoms of a kind, moving about as servants for the white Brazilians who worked them. It doesn't sound nearly as bad as the enslavement that other Africans were enduring, yet I suspect that if this were true, the situation might have continued to run smoothly for the remaining half-century until slavery was abolished in 1888. But again, things turned out differently.

In Bahia in January of 1835, shit kicked off. A revolt took place, quietly planned by the leaders of the community of enslaved black Muslims. It lasted three days, and was suppressed by the Brazilian authorities, but sent reverberations through the country. Fearing the bloodlust of another black Muslim uprising, the Brazilian government drew up a solution: get rid of them. Following the execution of the leaders of the revolt, who are said to have known of the success of the Haitian Revolution, it was decided that the community as a whole was not to be trusted. Anybody suspected of involvement was deported to West Africa, which is to say that it didn't matter whether they were involved or not.

From its birth in 1804 as a country independent of France, Haiti (from the Taíno-Arawak *Ay-ti, land of mountains*) was the first nation to permanently abolish slavery. This is true despite how often it is paraded that Britain led the way in outlawing the trade in African peoples in 1807, and later their ownership, in 1834. By 1835, the British were offering ships to carry formerly enslaved blacks to Africa. After compensating their own share of slave-owners to the tune of £20 million – £17 billion being the contemporary total finally paid by UK taxes in 2015 – perhaps a complimentary voyage was the least that could be offered.

Oral history has it that one such voyage from Bahia to Nigeria and then Ghana was made by the *S. S. Salisbury*. Stories differ as to the date of the trip in question but it is thought that the first arrival of returnees (refugees, essentially) occurred in 1829. Crucially, this is prior to the Malê

Revolt of 1835, but nonetheless foreshadows it: given the brutality of black life in Brazil, it is evidence that those who had an opportunity to leave did so. In the aftermath of the uprising were two more arrivals with passengers numbering in the hundreds, but on the first – that of 1829 – were seven families under the leadership of one figure. His name was Kangidi Asuman. Kangidi is a place name in Nigeria. Asuman relates not-so-distantly to the Arabic name, *Osman*.

But, at some point I am yet to know of, he dropped Kangidi. I can only speculate as to why. We must remember that when he was taken from wherever it was he originated – say, Kangidi – things could have happened there that changed it permanently. Slave raids and bounty huntings were bloody occurrences. Who is to say what was left of home, or that Kangidi-the-place even existed still. Perhaps he knew the answer to this because he saw it as he was taken: nothing. Towns do burn, after all.

Whatever the truth, Kangidi was no more. He dropped the name, kept Asuman, and added *Nelson*. Today, the male descendants of Asuman Nelson – the founding leader of the community known as the Tabom – still carry this name. Time doing what it does, however, the spelling has since changed.

*

One of my co-fellows at the residency in Bahia is Amira, an African American dancer and Lucumí priestess from Oakland, California, with a face that looks a lot like my mother's. She has been visiting and working in Brazil for years, since a long-ago relationship with someone from here. Like me, she has looked into her lineage, and it happens that she believes she is of Ghanaian heritage. On more than one of our trips by ferry into mainland Salvador, as we browse stores and markets, strangers assume we are related. *She is your daughter?* they ask in Portuguese and, only half jokingly, Amira says *yes*.

*

The song 'The Waters of March' refers in part to a season in Brazil when it begins to rain. Brazil is on the southern hemisphere, which means that the seasons are the other way around to how they are here, on the northern side. As we enter winter, they enter summer. As they leave autumn, we leave spring. As I write this, in London, it is March; just days from my birthday. Trees are in bloom, and we are indoors – because it is the time of coronavirus. But it is spring, nonetheless, even without us.

In Brazil, March is the onset of autumn. At this time, it rains heavily. Sometimes for days on end. For us, at the residency in Bahia, this manifests as three days of thunder and downpour, before a sudden stop. Finally able to step out again, Amira, myself and some others decide to go back to the holy water place to see if it has been restored by the wet weather. When we get there, there is a small pool. Amira crouches down, unties her hair, and scoops handfuls of water over her head. She sits back a moment, stares out and sobs, quietly. I watch, not knowing quite what to do, but saddened also. I touch her shoulder without knowing if I should. When this is over, she touches the water again and this time, sings. I don't understand, but I know she is singing in Yoruba and saying, at times, *iya mi*, which I know means *my mother*. I know that one of her divinities in Lucumí is Oshun, a feminine divinity of fresh waters. Amira takes a bottle of honey out of her backpack, and pours it tenderly into the small clear pool, cooing lullaby-like as one would to something beloved, repeating at times the words I know, *iya mi, iya mi...*

*

Every now and then for years after I learn of the Tabom and my descent, through my mother, from one of their founding figures, I will enter the name *Nelson* into Facebook or Instagram search boxes, and scan for black faces. The last time I will do this, I will reach out to someone who, like me, lives in London. An *Azumah Nelson*. He will reply and confirm that he does indeed share this heritage, but that what he knows of it is limited.

Perhaps a year or so later, before I leave for Brazil to research this history, he will message to wish me well. When I am back, I will cross paths with him at a magazine launch for which I am reading poems. This is the first time we will meet. When he greets me, I won't know who he is, and it will take me more than a moment to understand. He will be tall. In another moment, Kareem, a mutual friend of ours, will grab us both and marvel that we know each other. And I will think, but not say: *I don't know him. We don't know each other, not really.* The three of us will laugh about the sea of whiteness in the room and the subtext of how glad we are to have found each other here. Someone else I know will then pull my attention, and the rest of the moment will be lost.

Nearly two years later, we will meet again. This time, at the surprise birthday party of Belinda, the friend with whom I will have travelled back from a literary festival in Lagos, days earlier. On that trip, Belinda and I had feared that the boat ride to the beach would kill us. The boat had stopped numerous times, mid-water, overloaded, its rudder tangled with weeds. We had both pondered our drownings; the absence of our deaths' reportage on the news. Before Belinda will arrive to singing and loud joy, Caleb and I will talk. He will be a writer, like myself, and quiet. Surprise party duties at hand, we will exchange details and agree to catch up another time. He will message days later, to ask when I am free, and I will be free on a Thursday. We will meet in Bethnal Green for tea, from which point we will become friends, and swap books, and keep in touch.

*

In the living room of the flat I share with T is a bookcase built into the alcove of the wall. It is sectioned off into parts, most of which are filled by the books I brought here when I left my parents' house. The central section of the bookcase is empty of books, though. Here, instead, are a number of things: a bracelet of cowrie shells; a selection of semi-precious stones; a handful of sand grabbed in haste the day I left the island of Itaparica in Bahia; a candle, usually; a miniature wooden sculpture of an elephant, from Accra; Florida Water of the kind that was sprinkled at my grandmother's grave, a year on from her death; a bell; and an image, cut from his obituary, of my grandfather and my grandmother on what looks like their wedding day. Last of all, there is a shot glass, not mine but taken from the room at my parents' house that I shared with my older sister. I won't say I stole it because it never seemed needed, and it was left behind when she moved out.

I keep this shot glass filled with fresh water as best I can. Sometimes, which means less often than I wish to, I stand in front of this display on a morning and light the candle, and ring the bell. And then I talk.

I make a greeting in Ga, my parents' language, my language – even though I cannot speak it. I say *thank you* for some things, and say *please help* for others, and then I say *thank you* again. I talk, clumsily, a little unsure, but earnestly for a short while, and then I finish, snuffing the candle out between two fingers. Sometimes when I stand there, I worry that I am only speaking to myself, but I keep going anyway. Sometimes, I know that I am not.

    This is what faith looks like to me.

*

I have been trying to write about water but I keep getting caught up; keep finding the pool empty, the spring out of reach or dry. In my mind, *to write* is a verb formation similar to that of *to grasp*, so therefore, yes, it's true: I would like to write about something that can barely be held in two hands. Imagine a thing such as that. But we're here now, so suppose the superior verb is *grapple*. It has grit in it. Torque, if you will. So now: let's go. When grappling, the tendency is to grapple *with*, which is suggestive of a residual division between two entities, each one retaining its selfhood. A sacred space between that which captures and that which is caught. Predator and prey. This feels apt. There is something in it. *Grapple*. Slight consonance with rubble. Which makes me now think of ruin. *Ruinous*. Assonance with *apple*. Ruinous, again; that first illicit fruit. You know how the rest of it goes. One small bite for man that wasn't so small at all. Knowledge of good and evil thereafter and – wait a minute – as a word, what use could *good* ever have been against evil when it has such holes in it. Two eyes wide in shock, as though they died that way, or watch on, astounded, still. This also feels apt. And so, I grapple. I am trying to do this with water, but even this word will neither contain nor cut it. I test the image in my head and resurface with the conviction that a floor cloth will be needed at some point after a mess has been made. Ruinous, these fragments, yes. Where is the floor cloth for history? Where is the shore of its ruin?

    Writing about water is possibly only minimally less hard than writing about air. *What does it smell like? How does it taste? Is it safe to take in?* And while I'm circling around the sense of how alike water is to language – as characterised by its slippage as it is by its force – why don't I also say that insofar as it is not easily contained, writing *about* it sounds equally impossible. I am less able to encompass water than it is capable of encompassing me. And I can't swim. If I wade in beyond my nose, I may not survive. I should learn, it's true – and soon, at that – but maybe swimming is not something I must do here, now. It is possible that I need only to be calm. Un-tense my limbs, and breathe in, diaphragm-deep and babylike, easy. *How it's good, so good.* I might be buoyed and carried somewhere I haven't been before. Another archipelago of being. A place as yet unnamed. *Don't despair.*

ANNA ASLANYAN is a freelance journalist and translator from Russian. She writes for the *London Review of Books*, the *Times Literary Supplement* and other publications. Her popular history of translation, *Dancing on Ropes: Translators and the Balance of History*, will be published by Profile in May 2021.

EMILY BERRY is the author of two poetry collections, *Dear Boy* (2013) and *Stranger, Baby* (2017), both from Faber. She edits *The Poetry Review*. *Many Nights*, a photobook featuring Jacqui Kenny's pictures and the complete version of 'The Secret Country of her Mind', will be published in 2021.

VICTORIA ADUKWEI BULLEY is a poet, writer and filmmaker. She is the recipient of an Eric Gregory Award, and has held artistic residencies internationally in the US, Brazil and at the V&A Museum in London. A Complete Works and Instituto Sacatar fellow, her pamphlet *Girl B* (*Akashic*) forms part of the 2017 New-Generation African Poets series. She is a doctoral student at Royal Holloway, University of London, where she is the recipient of a Technē studentship for doctoral research in Creative Writing.

FIONA ALISON DUNCAN is a Canadian-American author and artist. Her debut novel *Exquisite Mariposa* won the 2020 LAMBDA Literary Prize for Bisexual Fiction.

LAURA ELLIOTT is a poet and library worker in London. She is the author of *this is hunting* (Distance No Object, 2019), *rib-boning* (Moot Press, 2019), and *lemon, egg, bread* (Test Centre, 2017). She co-edits the experimental poetry magazine *para·text* with Angus Sinclair.

CORA GILROY-WARE is a multidisciplinary artist. She writes music and performs under the name Fauness, and teaches History of Art at the University of York.

HERVÉ GUIBERT (1955–91) was a French writer and photographer. He was the author of some thirty books and played a significant role in changing public attitudes in France toward AIDS. Hervé Guibert died at the age of 36 in Paris following a failed suicide attempt.

ILYA LEUTIN was born in Siberia in 1986. He is a screenwriter and a columnist for a number of Russian publications, including *Snob* and *The Russian Muslim*. The pieces in this issue come from his first book, *Ravshan's Real Stories*, published in 2012 under the name Ravshan Saleddin. It was longlisted for the National Bestseller award and shortlisted for the Russian Debut prize. He is also the author of the novel *Silence Full Blast* (2015) and the collections *The Caramel Knight* (2016) and *Oriental Miniatures* (2018).

BENOÎT LOISEAU is a writer and critic based primarily in London. His writing has appeared in *Frieze*, the *Financial Times* and the *Guardian*, among others. He is a doctoral researcher at the University of Edinburgh, where he also teaches.

JULIAN LUCAS is a writer and critic based in Brooklyn.

CALEB AZUMAH NELSON is a 26-year-old British-Ghanaian writer and photographer living in south-east London. His writing has been published in *Litro*. He was recently shortlisted for the Palm Photo Prize and the BBC National Short Story Prize 2020, and won the People's Choice prize. His debut novel, *Open Water*, is out next year.

ELIZABETH O'CONNOR lives and works in Birmingham. She recently received her PhD in modernist poetry, and is interested in writing about natural history, animals and plants. She is the winner of The White Review Short Story Prize 2020.

ADAM PENDLETON (b. 1984, Richmond, Virginia) is recognised for his conceptual practice, which encompasses painting, sculpture, writing, film, and performance. He has been the subject of solo exhibitions across the United States and abroad, at institutions including the Indianapolis Museum of Contemporary Art (2008); Kunstverein, Amsterdam (2009); The Kitchen, New York (2010); the Contemporary Arts Center, New Orleans, the Museum of Contemporary Art, Denver and the Museum of Contemporary Art Cleveland, Ohio (2016); Kunst-Werke Institute for Contemporary Art, Berlin (2017); Baltimore Museum of Art (2017).

INGRID POLLARD is a British artist and photographer. In 2018 she was the Stuart Hall Associate Fellow at the University of Sussex.

BRANDON TAYLOR is the author of the novel *Real Life*, which was a New York Times Editors' Choice and shortlisted for the 2020 Booker Prize. His work has appeared in *Guernica*, *American Short Fiction*, *Gulf Coast*, *The New York Times*, *The New Yorker* online, *The Literary Review* and elsewhere. He holds graduate degrees from the University of Wisconsin-Madison and the Iowa Writers' Workshop, where he was an Iowa Arts Fellow.

JENNIFER LEE TSAI is a poet, editor and critic. She was born in Bebington and grew up in Liverpool. A fellow of The Complete Works and a Ledbury Poetry Critic, her work features in the Bloodaxe anthology *Ten: Poets of the New Generation* (2017). She is a Contributing Editor at *Ambit*. Her debut poetry pamphlet is *Kismet* (ignitionpress, 2019). Currently, she is an AHRC PhD Researcher in Creative Writing at the University of Liverpool. She is the winner of a Northern Writers Award for Poetry 2020.

JACK UNDERWOOD's double pamphlet *Solo for Mascha Voice/Tenuous Rooms* was published by Test Centre in 2018. *Happiness* was published by Faber & Faber in 2015. He is senior lecturer in creative writing at Goldsmiths, University of London.

PLATES

Cover   Ingrid Pollard, from *Landscape Trauma*, 2001, digital print on stretched synthetic canvas, 310 × 252 cm. Courtesy the artist. © Ingrid Pollard.

p. 11   Caleb Azumah Nelson, *Nimble*, 2019, digital print, 204.8 × 263 cm. Courtesy the artist.

I   Hervé Guibert, *Michel Foucault*, 1981, gelatin silver print, 16.8 × 11.4 cm. Courtesy the Estate of Hervé Guibert, Paris, and Callicoon Fine Arts, New York.

II   Hervé Guibert, *Le Table de Travail*, 1989, gelatin silver print, 14 × 21.6 cm. Courtesy the Estate of Hervé Guibert, Paris, and Callicoon Fine Arts, New York.

III   Hervé Guibert, *New York*, 1981, gelatin silver print, 14.3 × 21.9 cm. Courtesy the Estate of Hervé Guibert, Paris, and Callicoon Fine Arts, New York.

IV   Hervé Guibert, *Sienne*, 1979, gelatin silver print, 16.5 × 25.4 cm. Courtesy the Estate of Hervé Guibert, Paris, and Callicoon Fine Arts, New York.

V   Hervé Guibert, *Thierry Do*, n.d, gelatin silver print, 15.2 × 23.5 cm. Courtesy the Estate of Hervé Guibert, Paris, and Callicoon Fine Arts, New York.

VI   Hervé Guibert, *Santa Caterina, panier de fraises*, 1990, gelatin silver print, 14.6 × 21.9 cm. Courtesy the Estate of Hervé Guibert, Paris, and Callicoon Fine Arts, New York.

VII   Hervé Guibert, *Autoportrait avec Suzanne et Louise*, 1979, gelatin silver print, 14.6 × 22.9 cm. Courtesy the Estate of Hervé Guibert, Paris, and Callicoon Fine Arts, New York.

VIII   Hervé Guibert, *Isabelle*, 1980, gelatin silver print, 14.6 × 21.9 cm. Courtesy the Estate of Hervé Guibert, Paris, and Callicoon Fine Arts, New York.

IX   Hervé Guibert, *Autoportrait*, 1989, gelatin silver print, 21.9 × 14.3 cm. Courtesy the Estate of Hervé Guibert, Paris, and Callicoon Fine Arts, New York.

X   Hervé Guibert, *Vincent couché*, 1988, gelatin silver print, 14.3 × 21.6 cm. Courtesy the Estate of Hervé Guibert, Paris, and Callicoon Fine Arts, New York.

XI   Hervé Guibert, *Le Fiancé III*, n.d, gelatin silver print, 14.9 × 22.9 cm. Courtesy the Estate of Hervé Guibert, Paris, and Callicoon Fine Arts, New York.

XII   Hervé Guibert, *Musée non identifié*, 1978, gelatin silver print, 16.5 × 24.1 cm. Courtesy the Estate of Hervé Guibert, Paris, and Callicoon Fine Arts, New York.

XIII   Hervé Guibert, *Grille T. (de près) S.C.*, 1982, gelatin silver print, 14.6 × 22.9 cm. Courtesy the Estate of Hervé Guibert, Paris, and Callicoon Fine Arts, New York.

XIV   Hervé Guibert, *Thierry Toilette dans la sacristie*, 1983, gelatin silver print, 15.2 × 23.5 cm. Courtesy the Estate of Hervé Guibert, Paris, and Callicoon Fine Arts, New York.

XV   Hervé Guibert, *Les billes*, 1983, gelatin silver print, 14 × 21.6 cm. Courtesy the Estate of Hervé Guibert, Paris, and Callicoon Fine Arts, New York.

p. 75   Jacqui Kenny, *Fighting Dogs - Peru*, 2017, screenshot. Courtesy Jacqui Kenny. © Google.
p. 79   Jacqui Kenny, *Bush Array - USA*, 2017, screenshot. Courtesy Jacqui Kenny. © Google.
p. 83   Jacqui Kenny, *White Horse - Kyrgyzstan*, 2017, screenshot. Courtesy Jacqui Kenny. © Google.
p. 87   Jacqui Kenny, *Pink and Blue House - Peru*, 2017, screenshot. Courtesy Jacqui Kenny. © Google.

XVI   Ingrid Pollard, from *Pastoral Interlude*, 1987, hand-tinted silver print, 50.8 × 60.7 cm. Courtesy the artist. © Ingrid Pollard.

XVII   Ingrid Pollard, from *Pastoral Interlude*, 1987, hand-tinted silver print, 50.8 × 60.7 cm. Courtesy the artist. © Ingrid Pollard.

XVIII   Ingrid Pollard, from *Near and Far*, 1998. Courtesy the artist. © Ingrid Pollard.

XIX   Ingrid Pollard, from *Self Evident*, 1995, light box, 50.8 × 50.8 cm. Courtesy the artist. © Ingrid Pollard.

XX   Ingrid Pollard, from *Boy Who Watches Ships Go By*, 2002, photographic emulsion on stretched canvas, 76.2 × 30.5 cm. Courtesy the artist. © Ingrid Pollard.

XXI   Ingrid Pollard, *The Cost of the English Landscape*, 2018/1989, various printed media and wood. Courtesy the artist. © Ingrid Pollard.

XXII   Ingrid Pollard, from *Working Images*, 2008. Courtesy the artist. © Ingrid Pollard.

XXIII   Ingrid Pollard, from *Working Images*, 2008. Courtesy the artist. © Ingrid Pollard.

XXIV   Ingrid Pollard, from *Oceans Apart*, 1991, hand-tinted silver print. Courtesy the artist. © Ingrid Pollard.

XXV   Adam Pendleton, *Untitled (A Victim of American Democracy)*, 2016, silkscreen ink and spray paint on canvas, 271.8 × 149.9 cm. Courtesy the artist and Pace Gallery. © Adam Pendleton.

XXVI   Adam Pendleton, *Untitled (A Victim of American Democracy)*, 2017, silkscreen ink and spray paint on canvas, 213.4 × 152.4 cm. Courtesy the artist and Pace Gallery. © Adam Pendleton.

XXVII   Adam Pendleton, *Untitled (WE ARE NOT)*, 2019, silkscreen ink on canvas, 243.8 × 304.8 cm. Courtesy the artist and Pace Gallery. © Adam Pendleton.

XXVIII   Adam Pendleton, *Untitled (WE ARE NOT)*, 2019, silkscreen ink and spray paint on canvas, 91.4 × 71.1 cm. Courtesy the artist and Pace Gallery. © Adam Pendleton.

XXIX   Adam Pendleton, *Untitled (Who We Are)*, 2019, silkscreen ink and spray paint on canvas, 243.8 × 175.3. Courtesy the artist and Pace Gallery. © Adam Pendleton.

XXX   Adam Pendleton, *Untitled (WE ARE NOT)*, 2020, silkscreen ink on canvas, 243.8 × 175.3 cm. Courtesy the artist and Pace Gallery. © Adam Pendleton.

XXXI   Adam Pendleton, *Black Dada (A/A)*, 2019, silkscreen ink on canvas, 243.8 × 193 cm. Courtesy the artist and Pace Gallery. © Adam Pendleton.

XXXII   Adam Pendleton, *Black Dada Drawing (A)*, 2018, silkscreen ink on canvas, 66.4 × 52.7 cm. Courtesy the artist and Pace Gallery. © Adam Pendleton.

XXXIII   Adam Pendleton, *Black Dada Drawing (B)*, 2018–19, silkscreen ink on canvas, 66.4 × 52.7 cm. Courtesy the artist and Pace Gallery. © Adam Pendleton.

XXXIV   Adam Pendleton, *Black Dada Drawing (C)*, 2018–19, silkscreen ink on canvas, 66.4 × 52.7 cm. Courtesy the artist and Pace Gallery. © Adam Pendleton.

XXXV   Adam Pendleton, *Black Dada Drawing (D/D)*, 2018, silkscreen ink on canvas, 66.4 × 52.7 cm. Courtesy the artist and Pace Gallery. © Adam Pendleton.

There are *many dictionaries* for the tongue *I speak.*

— Zaffar Kunial, from 'Hill Speak' in *Us*

'One of Britain's
outstanding poets'
SIR PAUL McCARTNEY

'The velvet voice
of discontent'
KATE MOSS

'Nothing short
of dazzling'
ALEX TURNER

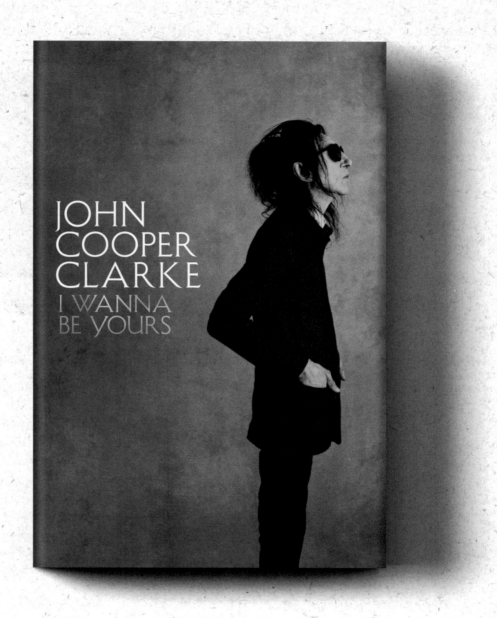

JOHN
COOPER
CLARKE
I WANNA
BE YOURS

The long-awaited memoir from John Cooper Clarke is out now.

PICADOR

VERSO
FICTION

We are delighted to add to our newly launched Verso Fiction imprint this season, with two stunning novels from Vigdis Hjorth and Jenny Hval.

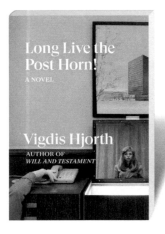

Long Live the Post Horn!
VIGDIS HJORTH
Translated by Charlotte Barslund

"A brilliant study of the mundane, full of unexpected detours and driving prose ... Hjorth's novel ingeniously orbits the intimate stories that are possible only when a character has put words on paper and sent them through the post" New York Times

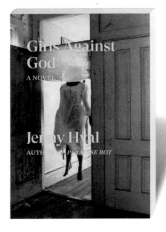

Girls Against God
JENNY HVAL
Translated by Marjam Idriss

From the author of the acclaimed *Paradise Rot*, Jenny Hval's latest novel is a radical fusion of feminist theory and experimental horror, and a unique treatise on magic, gender and art.

ALSO OUT THIS AUTUMN:

The Verso Book of Feminism
Revolutionary Words from Four Millennia of Rebellion
Edited by JESSIE KINDIG

An unprecedented collection of feminist voices from four millennia of global history; *The Verso Book of Feminism* is a weapon, a force, a lyrical cry, and an ongoing threat to misogyny everywhere.

A Kick in the Belly
Women, Slavery and Resistance
STELLA DADZIE

"An essential corrective to centuries of sublimation and the presentation of black women who lived through this history [slavery] as passive victims. I cannot recommend it highly enough." Bernardine Evaristo, author of *Girl, Woman, Other*

See more at Versobooks.com